He wasn't here to notice the woman.

He was here to get his son. And he could easily roll over, grab Gena Malone by the leg and end this standoff right now. But he wouldn't do that. He might be lower than a snake's belly at times, but he wasn't one to hurt women. Even the woman who'd kept his son hidden from him.

He'd have to figure out a way to get through the woman before he could take Scotty, because it was obvious this woman loved this child. And that meant she wouldn't let Scotty go without a fight.

"Okay, let's start over," he said. "I'm Eli Trudeau. And you are obviously the lovely, mysterious Gena. Since Devon handpicked you to raise my son, you can't be all bad."

Her boot put a little more pressure on his solar plexus. "And since he asked me to keep Scotty safe because he didn't trust you to raise him, you can't be all good."

"Ouch, that hurt." Eli used humor to hide the real hurt her words inflicted. And thought to himself that maybe she was right. "I've changed."

She stared at him.

Books by Lenora Worth

Love Inspired Suspense

Fatal Image
Secret Agent Minister
A Face in the Shadows
Deadly Texas Rose
Heart of the Night

Love Inspired

The Wedding Quilt
Logan's Child
I'll Be Home for Christmas
Wedding at Wildwood
His Brother's Wife
Ben's Bundle of Joy
The Reluctant Hero
One Golden Christmas
When Love Came to Town
Something Beautiful
Lacey's Retreat
Easter Blessings
"The Lily Field"

Steeple Hill

After the Storm
Echoes of Danger
Once Upon a Christmas
"'Twas the Week
    Before Christmas"

**The Carpenter's Wife*
**Heart of Stone*
**A Tender Touch*
Blessed Bouquets
"The Dream Man"
†A Certain Hope*
†A Perfect Love*
†A Leap of Faith*
Christmas Homecoming
Mountain Sanctuary
Lone Star Secret

*In the Garden
**Sunset Island
†Texas Hearts

LENORA WORTH

has written more than thirty novels, most of those for Steeple Hill Books. She also works freelance for a local magazine, where she has written monthly opinion columns, feature articles and social commentaries. She also wrote for five years for the local paper. Married to her high school sweetheart for thirty-three years, Lenora lives in Louisiana and has two grown children and a cat. She loves to read, take long walks and sit in her garden.

Heart of the Night

Lenora Worth

Steeple Hill®

Published by Steeple Hill Books™

STEEPLE HILL BOOKS

Steeple
Hill®

Recycling programs
for this product may
not exist in your area.

ISBN-13: 978-0-373-44321-5
ISBN-10: 0-373-44321-8

HEART OF THE NIGHT

www.SteepleHill.com

Printed in U.S.A.

And he said to them, Come away by yourselves to a desolate place and rest a while.

—*Mark* 6:31

To all the people of Grand Isle, Louisiana.
You are forever in my heart.

ONE

"I've come for my son."

The man holding a big battered hand over her mouth had a funny but familiar accent. He smelled of snow and wind, as if he'd been out in the night for a long time. His breath was warm as it fanned her ear and caused the hair on the back of her neck to stand up. His big body was broad and solid as he pulled her against him.

Gena tried to wiggle away, but he held her with an iron grip. So she closed her eyes, her heart rate accelerating as she became trapped in her worst nightmare.

She'd been expecting him.

"I'm not going to hurt you," the man said, his words as soft as silk. "I'll let you go if you promise not to scream. I don't want to frighten *him*."

Gena didn't want to scare her son either. So she nodded and waited for Eli Trudeau to release her.

And then she grabbed underneath the massive arm that had been restraining her and with a grunt and a prayer, she tripped Eli and flipped him over and onto the floor in a perfect takedown. He landed hard on his back with her booted foot centered on his belly.

Eli lay stunned for a few seconds, then let out a groan

as he shook his head to clear it. "For sure, I should have known Devon would train you in self-defense. But did you have to try and break my back?"

"Did you have to break into my home just to see your son?"

Well, at least she got right to the point. He liked that in a woman. Even the woman who'd been secretly raising his little boy.

He watched her breath coming fast and furious. "Can you let me up?" he asked in a nice way, with a nice smile, hoping she'd fall for it.

She didn't. "Why should I let you up? And why should I care that your back might be broken?"

Eli stayed still, the pressure of her boot somewhere near his spleen reminding him that he wasn't dealing with a girly-girl here. Gena Malone meant business. But then, so did he.

He carefully ticked off the facts inside his head, just to calm himself so he wouldn't do something stupid like grab her and pin her down, tie her up, then rush to his son's side.

Gena Malone Thornton. Thirty and widowed. Husband was a CHAIM agent who had been killed somewhere in Europe doing his duty for the Christian organization three months after they'd gotten married. Gena now lived in Maine in this cottage by the Atlantic Ocean and worked from home as a Web page designer. She also rented out two nearby cottages to make extra money.

While she dared him to move, Eli noticed how pretty she was. Her hair was curly and thick and dark, just like Scotty's. He couldn't be sure, but he'd guess her eyes were a deep blue like her brother's. She looked healthy—more curvy than slender in her jeans and long sweater. And lethal in the protective mama mode, no doubt.

Cut that out, Eli told himself. He wasn't here to notice the woman. He was here to get his son. And he could easily roll over, grab her by the leg and end this standoff right now. But he wouldn't do that. He might be lower than a snake's belly at times, but he wasn't one to hurt a woman. Even the woman who'd been raising his son.

But he'd have to figure out a way to get through the woman before he could see Scotty, because it was obvious this woman loved his child. And that meant she wouldn't let Scotty go without a fight. Eli should know; he'd sat in the broom closet for over an hour, watching her with Scotty. He'd just have to charm his way into getting what he'd come here for, he reckoned.

"Okay, let's start over," he said as he lifted his head. "I'm Eli Trudeau. I just happened to be in the neighborhood and thought I'd stop by to see *my* son. And you are obviously the lovely, mysterious Gena. Since Devon handpicked you to raise the boy, you can't be all bad."

Her boot put a little more pressure on his stomach. "And since he and I made a promise to each other to keep Scotty safe because he didn't trust *you* to raise him, you can't be all that good."

"Ouch, that hurt." Eli used humor to hide the real hurt her words inflicted and thought to himself that maybe she was right. "I've changed," he said, trying to hold up his hands in defense. "Honestly."

"How did you get in?" she asked, not moving and obviously not convinced. "Because I don't recall inviting you and because I have a pretty good alarm system."

"Part of the training," he shot back. "Your system wasn't good enough to stop me. What does it matter? I'm here now and we've been properly introduced, so could I have a cup of coffee at least? And maybe a sandwich? I'm sure hungry."

She pressed her boot against bone while she mulled over that request. But she sighed. "I'm going to let you up, because I believe underneath that black heart you have a good soul. But if you try anything, you just might live to regret it."

"I believe you, *chère,*" he said. "I won't cause any trouble. I don't want to upset the boy."

She lifted her foot. "Get up very slowly."

Eli did as she told him, biding his time for now. He stared up at the woman who'd just brought him down with a single swift move, his gaze slamming into hers as she gave him a look that floored him more than any physical moves ever could. It was a look full of anger and fear, a look that told him he might have to rethink taking the child away from the mother.

"Nice to meet you, Gena," he said, shooting her one of his winning smiles. "Can we talk?"

Gena circled him, her hands on her hips. "That depends. Do you think you can behave like a civilized human being?"

"Never tried that, but I reckon now's a good time to start, *oui?*"

She leaned over him, her long hair falling like black ribbons across her blue wool sweater. "I would suggest you be very careful. I have lots of weapons in this house and I know how to use all of them. You might have figured out how to turn off the alarm system, but you won't be able to figure out how to trick me, understand?"

Eli held up his hands in defeat, even though he was pretty sure she had no weapons. "Okay, I got it. We'll both make nice…for the boy's sake." Then he gave her what he hoped was a sincere stare because he meant what he was saying. "For my son's sake."

Gena reached out her hand to him. Eli took it and felt the pull of her strength all the way to his bones, along with what might be called an electric charge of awareness that reminded him of the mists he used to see in the marshes back in Louisiana. But he was so cold and stiff from hiding in that freezing closet that he couldn't be sure. He hated the cold.

"I'll make coffee and food," she said, her eyes never leaving his face as she backed up toward the counter. Then she pointed to one of the high-backed chairs by the table. "Sit. And don't make me regret this."

"Yes, ma'am," Eli said with a salute. "It's sure gonna be a long night."

She slammed cabinet doors and opened drawers. "You should have considered that before breaking into my home."

"I should have considered a whole lot of things," Eli retorted. "Especially you. *Most* especially you."

She turned and nodded. "You got that right, Disciple." Giving him a look that dismissed him, she added, "So you just sit right there and think this thing through before you make any more stupid mistakes."

He couldn't come up with a reply for that one. Finally, he said, "I watched you with the boy earlier."

She hissed a breath as she went still. "For how long?"

"Long enough. You need a comfortable chair in that closet." He shrugged. "Make the coffee and then we'll have a long talk. And I won't try anything…uh…stupid."

She whirled around, silent and stealth, a bit shaken— and very intimidating for a woman—while Eli remembered the first time he'd seen his son about an hour ago. His heart had hammered with each breath as he'd sat silent and still inside the tiny broom closet, the words screaming inside his head forcing him to inhale with slow, deliberate calculation. *I have a son. I have a son.*

When the time was right, he would make his move. Until then…well…Eli was learning patience. And sitting in that closet had given him plenty of time to practice it.

He'd been tired and cold and starving for a good meal when he'd broken in earlier, but he'd been starving for any glimpse of his son even more. So he'd reset the alarm, then waited and watched until he'd heard them arriving through the back door in a gush of freezing fresh air, their happy laughter tearing at his gut like a fish knife as Gena had looked around after her son giggled.

"What's so funny?" she asked. Eli was amazed at how such a swelling of maternal love filled her eyes each time she looked at Scotty.

"You are, Mommy," Scotty said, thick dark curls spraying out of control across his forehead. "You were humming."

"Was I?" Gena asked, turning to hand Scotty his mug of hot chocolate. "I don't recall. What was I humming?"

Scotty blew on the marshmallow Gena dropped into his hot chocolate, then grabbed an oatmeal cookie from the plate she had set on the small oak breakfast table.

"That song you like—from the Christmas play at church," Scotty replied just before he slurped his drink.

"What Child Is This?" Eli had recognized the song when he'd heard her humming it.

Gena squinted, then nodded. "I guess I was. It's one of my all-time favorites." She sat down beside her son, ran her fingers through his unruly curls, then took a bite of cookie. "I like that particular song because it was playing the night…the night you came into my life."

Scotty grinned. "I'm a December baby, right?"

"Right you are." Gena glanced at the magnetic calendar on the refrigerator. "You have a birthday coming up, too, don't you?"

Scotty bobbed his head. "Four more days. I like having my birthday on Christmas Eve. Me and Jesus get to celebrate together."

Gena laughed at that innocent comparison, while Eli, alternatively sweating and freezing in the closet, held his eyes tightly shut so he could tamp down the pain. He'd missed his son's birth.

"Jesus was born in a manger on a very special night. That's what the hymn I like is all about."

"He came to save us from our sins," Scotty said, reciting what he'd obviously learned in Sunday school. Then the very astute little boy asked, wide-eyed and curious, "What did I come to do, Mommy?"

Eli's breath hissed as he heard his son's innocent question. Restraining himself, he sent up another prayer for quiet and patience. Lydia Cantrell, soon to be Lydia Malone when she became the wife of his friend and fellow CHAIM associate Devon Malone, had shown Eli how to pray. She'd also shown him how to forgive. He was still working on both.

But hearing his son speak brought out all of Eli's long-held resentment—resentment toward his grandfather, toward his well-meaning friend Devon and toward God. *I should have been here,* Eli thought as he watched the woman and the boy. *I should have been here.* He shifted, his calf muscles screaming as he sat crouched in his hiding spot. The mother had told the child to change for bed, but the boy, *his son,* hadn't wanted to go just yet. He watched as they'd gone about their business—normal and loving and cozy. Eli was so tired of watching.

Gena made coffee for the man she had dreaded seeing for close to six years. And yet, she'd known he'd come one day. She'd felt it in her bones all winter long.

"Mommy!"

Gena's gaze locked with Eli's as she heard her son cry out. "I have to go to him. He's always hard to get to sleep."

Eli nodded, his expression solemn and unyielding. "I'll wait right here."

"You won't—"

"I won't do anything to upset either of you. I'll just get some of that good-smelling coffee." He nodded his head toward the hallway. "Go on now."

Breathing a sigh of relief, Gena hurried upstairs to Scotty's room, thinking that when she'd tucked Scotty in earlier, Eli had been hiding here the whole time. He had been right here, watching them. To keep herself from going into hysterics now while Eli's gaze followed her, she remembered her sweet son and how their nightly ritual had become so special, even if she did have to struggle with Scotty every night.

Rushing into his room, she found him sitting up and rubbing his eyes. "What's wrong, baby?"

"I had a bad dream."

Gena wished she was just having a bad dream, but this nightmare was very real. "It's okay. Try to go back to sleep."

"Can't I stay up and watch you work?"

"No, and I don't want to fight with you," Gena said as she tucked the cover back around him. "It's bedtime whether you like it or not. Now try to rest."

Scotty turned to her with a cute pout. "But soon it'll be winter break, remember?"

"I do remember," Gena replied, using her best stern mother tone. "But for now, it's late and we had a big night practicing for the Christmas play. It's already past your bedtime." *And your father is downstairs probably trying to figure out how to take you from me.*

"I don't wanna," Scotty said, his arms wrapped against his flannel action figure-inspired pajamas. "I'm not tired."

"Scotty, you're going to stay in bed," Gena retorted, thinking it was mighty hard to resist her son's boyish charms. For just a fleeting moment, she wondered if Scotty got that from his real father. Eli's face flashed through her mind, reminding her of the constant worries that never left her thoughts now that he knew about his son. Those worries had tripled over the last hour. What did Eli think about his son, now that he'd seen him? And when would he make his move? Because she was sure he was going to do just that.

Based on what her brother Devon had told her, Eli, known as the Disciple, known to be a hot-headed Cajun, known to break all the rules, *would* show up here one day to not only see his son, but probably also to take him home to Louisiana. Now he was here; now that could happen. Gena closed her eyes, wondering how she'd react if Eli insisted on taking *her* son away. Scotty was her child now. He would always be hers. And she'd fight anyone who tried to dispute that. Even the mysterious, handsome man sitting in her kitchen. Especially that man.

"Are you saying a prayer, Mommy?" Scotty asked as he tugged on Gena's sweater. "Are you asking God to make me sleepy?"

Gena opened her eyes, then shook her head. "No, but that's not a bad idea. Do you feel sleepy yet?"

"Kinda," he said as he flopped back and then burrowed underneath the navy blue train-embellished comforter. "Will you read to me?"

"Don't I always?" Gena replied. She picked up several of his favorite books. "But only a couple of stories. I have to get some work done before I can go to bed myself, because unlike you, I am tired and sleepy."

She was far from sleepy, but she was very tired of always having to watch her back, of always wondering when the worse would come. *Dear God, help me. Help me.*

Gena read to him for a few minutes, noticing that he'd finally settled back down. Glancing over at him, she said, "You have droopy eyes, little man."

Scotty sank back on his pillows. "Christmas will be here soon, won't it?"

Gena kissed the top of his head. "Sooner, if you go to sleep. Now say your prayers and you'll wake up in a good mood."

She sat there, holding Scotty's hand in hers as she watched the snow falling softly just outside his checkered flannel curtains, her serenity shattered, her loneliness as cold and solid as the winter frost that clutched at her soul. She couldn't fall apart now. Scotty needed her to be strong. Eli needed her to be strong, too, whether he realized that or not.

Dear God, help me. Help me to prepare for the worst.

Gena's late husband, Richard, and her brother, Devon, both members of the elite Christian organization known as CHAIM, had taught her to always follow her instincts, to listen, to watch, to wait. To expect the best, but prepare for the worst. And right now, her instincts were shouting at her. She felt uneasy and at odds as she stared out into the snow-blanketed woods. She repeated her prayers as she kissed Scotty's forehead.

Help me to expect the best, while I prepare for the worst. I know he's hurting, Lord. Help me to help him. Please don't let him take my son.

Gena left her son only to find Eli waiting for her as she came back into the kitchen, that same fervent prayer racing through her mind.

"Is he okay?"

The quiet question left her even more confused. "He's fine. I think he's just excited about Christmas."

When Eli didn't respond, she whirled to find him staring at her, his eyes dark with a sad longing that tugged at her heart.

He sat like stone, his onyx eyes following her as she silently made him a sandwich. She didn't know why she was making him a sandwich. It just seemed like the right thing to do. Then she almost giggled. The man who'd come thousands of miles to break into her house and take her son had requested a sandwich. Maybe she was entertaining an angel unaware.

Then again, maybe not.

"I hate this cold," Eli said to break the static of the silence. He could hear her breathing, could hear the knife slicing across the bread and meat as she fixed things pretty on the plate. She was probably thinking about how to fix things pretty by jabbing that same knife in his heart.

"I like the cold," she said as she sat the plate in front of him, then brought him a fresh cup of coffee. "It makes me feel safe."

Eli grunted a retort as he inhaled the first bite of the big sandwich. The bread was hearty and homemade, the roast beef fresh and thinly sliced. But the cold only reminded him of his time in Ireland. Cold and damp, dark and desolate. He'd been in exile away from everything and everyone, an exile in his physical being and a deep, dark exile in his own mind. And that whole time, his son had been in exile, too, here in this remote little fishing village in Maine.

"I can hear the ocean hitting the rocks," he said between chews. "This water is different from my ocean." That eternal pounding echoed the pounding of his heart as it crashed against his chest.

"I've never been to Louisiana," she replied as she finally sat down across from him with her own cup of coffee. "And why are we making small talk?"

He took a long drink, the hot liquid burning his throat while her eyes burned him with an intense heat. But he made sure his next words were as soft and sweet as the marshmallows she'd left open on the table. "Oh, we've got plenty of time to talk about why I'm here, darlin'. 'Cause I'm not leaving until we have an understanding."

She slammed her cup down so hard that coffee sloshed out on the table. "What kind of understanding?"

Eli polished off the last of the food, then leaned forward, his hands on the table, his smile patient and calm. "Like I told you earlier, *chère*—I've come for my son. And I'm not leaving here without him."

TWO

"Why are you doing this, Eli? Why didn't you just ring the doorbell like a normal human being?"

Shadows colored his face as his voice went low and grainy. "Haven't you heard? I'm not like other people."

Gena hid the mortal fear beating like a ship's broken sail inside her heart. "What were you planning to do? Just grab him up in the middle of the night? Kidnap a little boy who doesn't even know you exist?"

His eyes went as black as a moonless night. "I should have done that, because your brother and you plotted the same thing when he was born. You didn't give me a say in the matter back then, so why should I be so kind and understanding now?"

Gena held to the warmth of her coffee cup, listening as the wind picked up outside. The tick-tock of the old grandfather clock in the hallway seemed to echo a warning through the still house, while the lights on the Christmas tree in the living room sparkled and twinkled right on cue. "Eli, we did what we had to do to protect Scotty. We didn't know how you'd react. You were in bad shape."

His expression grew stony as he kept his eyes on her.

"Let's recap. Devon held up our mission in South America because he was worried about me, worried that I couldn't finish the job after I went out on my own. But the mission went bad when we were compromised and a young girl was killed. I only wanted to be home in time for my child's birth, but someone wanted me dead." He stopped, his hand going flat on the table. "That someone—my own grandfather— came after my wife and my unborn child to punish me. I went berserk and tried to find them, but I was too late."

Gena watched as he lowered his head and swallowed. "I was too late." The pain etched on his face spoke of just exactly how far off the deep end he'd gone. But when he looked back up at her, he wore a mask of calm. "Because of that, I got sent to a retreat—to rest and regroup—as my superiors put it. Trapped in a desolate place while my pregnant wife lay in a coma. She died, Gena, but not before the baby was delivered. Devon decided to take the baby. My baby. I should have been told the truth. I should have had the chance to decide for myself."

Gena blinked back the tears forming in her eyes. "I'm so sorry, Eli. I know how it feels to lose someone you love."

"I'm sure you do. But do you know how it feels to be deceived and tricked by everyone you trusted?"

Gena shook her head. "Devon thought he was helping you by protecting your son."

He leaned forward. "I should have been the one protecting the boy. That's why I'm here now. I'm so afraid someone will come after him again." He sank back in his chair. "The way they did my wife."

Gena trembled at that thought. "Have you heard something? Tell me, Eli."

He shrugged. "It's just a feeling, *chère*."

Gena's pulse burned a beat through her temple. "You can't just come in here and say that. What do you know?"

"More than I knew back then," he retorted. "I know I have a son and now I'm going to take care of him, no matter what CHAIM thinks."

Figuring he was just trying to scare her, Gena reminded herself that she'd been the one watching over Scotty for a long time now. "And what would you have done back then, if you'd known? I think I can answer that. You went out on a vigilante mission and no one could locate you. And by the time they'd found you, it *was* too late. You were in no shape to do anything, and if you'd known, you would have come back—"

"Back to my wife and my child," he finished. "You don't know what I went through."

"I think I do," she said, compassion softening her words. "I lost my husband to CHAIM, remember?" She could talk of pain and longing, but she wouldn't give him any more ammunition to use against her. "That kind of pain paralyzes a person. You almost went mad with grief and anger. Devon wanted to protect you and Scotty. Maybe his motives weren't pure and maybe his reasoning was out of whack, but his heart was on your side. He agonized over his decision, but he was trying to help."

Eli slammed his hand down hard against the table. "You and Devon have no idea what agony is. No idea at all."

Gena didn't know how to reach him. Since the cold night her brother had called her all those years ago asking her to take in Scotty, she'd heard all about the Cajun from Louisiana. She knew the Disciple was the most dangerous of the whole CHAIM team, knew he hadn't joined CHAIM so much as a true believer, but as someone who only wanted to measure up to his absent father's heroic status. He'd only wanted to prove to his bitter grandfather that he was worthy. But Eli's heart had never been centered on the true cause of CHAIM, to help and protect Christians in danger through amnesty, intervention and ministry. Eli lived for the danger, but from what she'd heard, he sure didn't seem to live to serve Christ.

"Eli," she said, hoping to make him understand, "you've come so far. You survived a near-breakdown, a gunshot wound from your grandfather and…Lydia told me you've been studying your Bible and trying to find God's love in your life. So why are you doing this?"

He sat like a giant statue, his face chiseled in rock, his eyes shining with the hardness of unearthed coal. "I want my son with me. *I* never had the luxury of a father growing up. I want him with me, no matter what."

Gena cupped her hands together as if in prayer. "Do you hear yourself? No matter what? What does that mean, exactly? That you'll do whatever it takes to just pull him away from me, without any consideration for his feelings or mine? Did you even bother to think this through? Does Devon know you're here?"

"Devon has no right to stop me." He leaned back, frustration coloring his tanned skin as he raked a hand over his dark shaggy hair. "And let me see if I can answer your questions to your satisfaction. Number one—I've had plenty of time to consider everyone's feelings in this situation, including my own. Number two—I've had nothing else to think about since the night my grandfather died and I got shot—the night your brother informed me that I had a son. And number three—Dev does not know I'm here. That man is busy planning his wedding to Lydia. Why bother him with all the details of my torment and my shame?"

Gena put her hands on the table. "I need to call him."

Eli had her hands in his before she could get out of the chair and to the phone. "Do not call your brother. This is between me and you. Here, right now. That's why I left without telling him."

"You didn't tell him because you know what he would have said."

"You're right there, *belle*. I don't have to take orders from Devon Malone." He held her hands in his with an iron grip, but it wasn't a cruel hold. More like a plea for her to stop. "I'm not going to do anything to hurt you or the boy. I just wanted to…see him." His hands went soft over hers. "I just wanted to see him and make sure he was safe."

Tears pricked at Gena's eyes. She could see the love Eli had for Scotty there in the shadows around his dark eyes. She knew that same fierce love inside her heart. And she had no right to Scotty, no legal right. Eli could take him by force, or he could just take him. Period. How could she fight that? Worse, how could she fight the pain and torment this man had felt for the last few years? For all of his life.

"I won't call Devon yet," she finally said, the heat from his hands making her too aware of him. "But I can't let you take Scotty away from me. I can't. I love him so much. Please think about this. You can sleep on the couch tonight, and we'll talk again in the morning. But understand I'll be guarding him all night long."

She watched as his soul went into war. Gena could see it all there like a storm cloud on his face, the pain, the shame, the anger and then as the deep slashes of fatigue caught up with him, the resolve. "You don't have to guard the boy from me, *catin*. I am not a thief in the night. I'm just a father who wants to…know his son."

"I understand that and I want that for you," she said, a shudder of deep relief sliding down her spine. "If you'd like to stay here in Captive Cove for a while, I can let you have one of the other cottages. There's a small one right next door. It's yours for as long as you want."

"How about for a lifetime?" he said, the words a harsh whisper.

Gena didn't know how to respond to that question. This man was so different from anyone she'd ever met. He was like the night, dark and mysterious and dangerous. His clipped Cajun accent and the way he spoke the English language with such a colloquial French twist, made her heart do funny little things. Lydia had warned her about Eli. Not about the dangers inside the man, but about the vulnerable darkness that he tried so hard to hide. It was there now in his eyes, in his expression, in the way he sat staring at her like a caged, wounded animal.

And she had always had a soft spot for hurt creatures of any kind. "Eli, you can stay and get to know your son, but on my terms. All right?"

"Do I have any other choice?" he said, getting up to stalk to the sink. "Captive Cove! Now that is a fitting name for this place if ever there was one." Then he turned and came to tower over her. "But you need to understand one thing yourself. I'm only doing this your way for the boy's sake. Got that?"

She bobbed her head. "We can agree on that, at least."

He lifted a hand in the air. "Just give me the key to the cottage. I don't want to stay in here." He shrugged. "If he wakes up and finds me here, he'll have questions. Questions that should have been answered years ago."

Gena felt that jab toward her life here with Scotty hitting her with ice-pick precision. He resented her, but he had to tolerate her in order to see his son. She didn't know why that should hurt so much, but it did.

"I'll get the key," she said. "You'll find everything you need in the cottage—linens, some food staples, coffee and wood for a fire. We can get the rest when this storm clears up. Until then, you're welcome to have your meals here. And we'll explain things to Scotty after he's had time to get to know you."

He pulled his gaze away from her to stare out the window. "When will this weather clear?"

"I'm not sure. The weatherman predicted a lot of snow. It could be tomorrow or days from now."

He rolled his eyes, indignant with this confinement. Eli Trudeau was not a man to be locked away or shut inside. He looked like he belonged out in nature, walking, hunting, stalking, staring at the moon. He had a heart of the night.

Gena prayed she could bring some light into his battered soul.

Eli pushed his head back against the soft pillows on the old four-poster bed, then closed his eyes, memories of Leah moving like wind through his tired mind. He could see her there walking along the bayou behind their little house, her long blond hair falling away from her face, her hand on her already-protruding belly as she smiled down at the child she carried. But that vision was quickly replaced by the one he couldn't keep out of his mind, the one he could only imagine because he hadn't been there—the sight of his beautiful wife lying in a sterile hospital room hooked up to wires and tubes so that their child could stay alive long enough to be born.

Eli jerked his head up, wiping his eyes as if to get rid of the horror of that image. Staring into the crackling fire across the room, he thought, Do you know how much I loved you, *chérie?* Do you know that I would have fought all of them just to be by your side?

Too late now for that. But not too late for a chance to be a father to his son. And so he waited, hearing the clock strike midnight, hearing the gentle falling of snow all around the little house and the falling of the last burned log in the grate, hearing the ocean crashing madly against the shore. He waited and watched and listened as if he were on the most dangerous mission of his life. And maybe he was. He just had a bad feeling, a very bad feeling about things.

He wouldn't sleep. He knew that. He couldn't remember the last time he'd had a good night's sleep. Eli found no peace in his dreams or in his waking hours.

He'd traveled thousands of miles just to find his son, but his soul had traveled a long and rocky road just to find a little redemption. He's seen that redemption tonight, shining like a beacon in his son's dark eyes.

"Scotty," he said out loud. "What kind of name is that?" He tested it. "Scotty Trudeau."

Did they even let him go by the name Trudeau? Probably not. Scotty Malone? "Scotty," he said again into the darkness of the neat, comfortable room. The name echoed like a child's giggle against the walls.

Outside the wind howled and laughed, mocking Eli's attempts to wrap his mind around fatherhood. It was bitter cold, but he felt a hot sweat moving over his body like a fever. He gripped the patterned quilt on the bed, wondering if he was going back into that dark place inside his own head again.

"Can't go there," he reminded himself. "They'd force me to go back to Ireland." And he was not going back there, ever. How the Shepherd lived there was beyond Eli's comprehension, but at least his friend and fellow CHAIM agent had been kind when Eli had tried every trick in the book to break out of the ancient stronghold that had held him captive for months. "Retreat? More like a padded, emerald-green prison."

Pushing that time and those memories out of his mind, Eli tried to pray. He'd promised Lydia he would pray each time he got an urge to do something stupid—like leave New Orleans and come all the way up the coast in the middle of winter to see his son and make sure he was safe and sound. But his prayers were more of a haphazard merging of words. *Help. Hurt. Anger. Pain. Scotty. Scotty. Leah. Gena. Help me. Help them. Lord, help us all.*

Gena. She hated him. He had felt that hatred like clouds of swamp mosquitoes whirling around them earlier when she'd handed him the keys to this cozy cottage. And how could he blame her? She might hate him, but she surely loved his son. Her son.

His son.

"What now?" he asked himself. "How are you going to get out of this one?"

His cell phone rang. Not many had his number, so he figured this was urgent. When he saw Lydia's number flashing, he let out a sigh, then answered. "*Chère,* you are for sure like an old mother hen."

"Only because I love you," Lydia Cantrell said in her drawling Georgia accent. "Eli, Kissie called. She said you took off without saying goodbye, and she doesn't know where you went. Please tell me you didn't—"

"I didn't do anything crazy," he said, knowing what she was asking. And because he couldn't lie to Lydia, he said, "I'm in Maine, *ma petite*. I've seen the boy."

She whispered a soft prayer. "Oh, Eli. Why didn't you let us know you were going? You didn't scare Scotty, did you? You didn't do anything you'll regret, right?"

"I told you, it's cool. Everything is okay, except this infernal cold and snow. I hate cold and snow."

But Lydia was beyond listening to his complaints and well into her interrogation mode. The woman would have made a great CHAIM agent. "You didn't try to take him from Gena, did you?"

Skipping the part about disarming the alarm system and waiting in the broom closet, he said, "I thought about it, but Gena put me on my back and pinned me down until I cried 'uncle.'"

"Good for her. You know, she's trained in self-defense."

"You don't say? It's all right now, though. We talked pretty for a while and now I'm as cozy as a kitten in my little cottage by the sea." He shivered as he said that, his gaze hitting the dying embers of the fire.

"I hope so. Devon doesn't know I'm calling you, but I'll have to tell him. And I want to tell him you're being a gentleman. You promised me if you ever went to Maine, you'd only go to *visit* Scotty."

"I've been known to break my promises, *oui?*"

"You won't break this one," Lydia said in her smug, proud Lydia way. "I know you won't."

"You know me so well then?"

"I think I do. You want to make your son proud. You can do this, Eli. I'm praying you will."

"You might want to save those prayers, *catin*. I'm not

doing so good right now." He pinched his nose. "I want my son."

"Eli, don't talk like that. Think about how you'd confuse Scotty. You can't do that. He's a little boy. He doesn't understand. You have to take this slow."

"He doesn't know his father."

"It's hard, I know," she said, "but…you have to be very careful. You have to give Gena time to accept that you're there. And you have to be gentle with Scotty, okay?"

"I'm not a gentle man. And I'm not a *gentleman*."

"But you can be, you big brute. You can be. Will you try, for me?"

Eli got up to pace around the bedroom. "Ah, now, don't go laying that on me, Lydia. You know you are one of the few to sway my cold, hard heart."

"Then consider this my way of swaying," she said. "Do I need to call Devon and put him on you?"

"*Non.* I can't take his lectures tonight."

"Okay, then. We have an understanding. You are going to be a good father, Eli. No, make that a great father. I have faith in that. But first, you have to learn what being a father is all about."

Eli swallowed back the pride of hearing that from such a true Christian woman. "Why do you fight for me, Lydia?"

"Because you fought for me once, remember?"

"More like, I fought against you, trying to save your life."

"You did save my life and now it's my turn to save yours. I'm going to say prayers for you right now. Oh, and you'd better be here for our wedding in February."

"That is one promise I will keep. Sweet dreams, *mon amie,*" Eli said. "Tell Devon he is a lucky man."

"He's a blessed man," Lydia countered. "There's a difference."

Eli hung up with a smile, thinking she always had to have the last word.

"And I'm a blessed man, too, for knowing you," he said. But it would sure be hard living up to Lydia's sweet expectations.

Eli went to the big window next to the bed and opened the heavy curtain. He could see a single light burning upstairs in the big cottage where his son was sleeping. He wondered what it would be like to live there with Scotty, to watch his son laugh and cry, to play catch in the backyard, to go fishing out in that deep water. What would it be like to be a real father to Scotty?

"Only one way to find out," Eli said, smiling for the first time in a long time.

At least he knew Scotty was safe here tonight. That meant a lot to him even if he did resent his son being here. But what about tomorrow or the next day?

As he watched the house, a massive cloud moved over the water and turned the night a dark, moonless gray, causing shadows to dance against the tall trees and craggy rocks. A shudder clutched his spine like spider webs, sticky and unbreakable, trapping him with a new kind of fear. A little prickle of awareness and apprehension caused the hairs on his neck to stand up. He went from fatigued and worn out to wide awake and on full alert.

What if Eli's worries came to pass? What if Scotty *wasn't* safe here? What then?

THREE

"Look out your kitchen window."

Eli stood in the small den, watching the house across the snow-covered yard. When Gena appeared looking wary and surprised at the window a few feet away, he waved to her. "Is the boy up yet?"

"He has a name," she said, her voice low. "You can't keep calling him the boy, you know."

"Is my son up yet?" Eli retorted, his voice gravelly. He had not slept well, but then he never slept well.

"He's getting dressed for school."

"I'll take him. Give me directions."

"No, you will not take him. You're a stranger to him, Eli. Just give me some time to figure out how to handle this."

Eli let out a sigh, his eyes scanning the yard. In the light of a crisp white morning, this place looked serene and peaceful, as if it'd been purposely set up for a Christmas card. But it hadn't seemed that way late in the wee hours when he'd seen every shadow and shape as something sinister and dangerous. He didn't like this antsy feeling that had brought him here, but he was glad he'd followed his instincts.

"I'm coming over," he said, disconnecting and moving

away from the window before she could respond. He did turn in time to see the frustration on her face.

Let her be frustrated. He wanted to get to know his son, but more importantly, he wanted to protect his son. Because he hadn't been there when his wife and child had needed him the most. That reality ate at him day and night, always. But he was here now.

Closing his eyes to the dark, swirling memories, Eli took another swig of coffee and wished he had some strong Louisiana coffee instead. This brew would have to suffice for now. He grabbed his coat and headed out across the crunchy snow, noticing the vulnerability of this quiet cove. A sheer drop of cliffs off into a frigid ocean on one side and a copse of trees that blocked the view to the road on the other. Not good, not good at all. He felt an urgent need to get his son out of here, but he reminded himself Scotty had been safe here for six years.

But that didn't matter in Eli's eyes. He'd heard some rumblings when he'd been down in New Orleans recovering from being shot. Since the news of his grandfather's involvement in a South American drug cartel had come to light this summer, he'd felt deep in his bones that more trouble was on the way. His instincts had never let him down before, not even after Leah had disappeared six years ago and he'd gone off the deep end. Not even after CHAIM officials had forced him to go into confinement in Ireland for a few years to cool off and get his head straight, and not after he'd left and come home only to find out someone wanted him dead. That someone had been his own estranged grandfather. His instincts had been right on all those accounts, starting with the bad feeling he'd gotten when the team had first hit the ground in South America all those years ago. And things had gone very wrong down there. Eli had the distinct feeling that the situation still wasn't all cleaned up and tidied.

The Peacemaker would have seen to that.

Even though the Peacemaker was dead and buried and his South American crime group dissolved, the man had probably left henchmen everywhere to carry on his dirty deeds. And if the Peacemaker's cohorts had any inkling that he had a great-grandson…well, Eli didn't want to think about that. What if someone, somewhere, was just biding time, waiting to make a move on him or his child?

Maybe Dev was right, he thought as he knocked on the front door. As long as Eli had been out of the picture and tucked away in that retreat in Ireland, Scotty had been relatively safe. But once Eli had reappeared on the CHAIM radar last summer, he'd also set himself up for retribution from past enemies because he'd never been one to win friends and influence people. And now that meant his son could become a target. Somehow, he'd have to make Gena see that Scotty was better off with him.

But when she opened the door hard enough to shake the bright red ribbon on the fragrant evergreen wreath, a brooding frown on her pretty oval face, Eli got the impression that Gena wouldn't listen to any worries he might have.

Gena was fully prepared to slam the door back in Eli's too-good-looking-for-his-own-good face, but knowing her son was about to come barreling down the stairs, she didn't do that. This was Scotty's father, after all. And in spite of her sleepless night, Scotty and Eli both deserved a chance to get to know each other.

"What did you tell him?" Eli said as he muscled past

her, then pivoted to glare at her. "I mean, about his father? Does he even ask?"

Gena glanced upstairs, then motioned toward the kitchen. "I never lied to him, if that's what you're asking. I have always told him that his father had to go away and that he might not be able to come back." She looked down at the floor. "He held out hope, I think, that one day he would see his father."

Eli thumped his fingers on the newel post. "Well, guess what, *catin,* I'm here now. Time to confess all."

Gena's heart did a little pulsing jump. "Eli, please?"

Before she could plead her case, Scotty called out, "I'm hungry, Mom. Did you make pancakes?"

Gena stopped in the entryway, her gaze locking with Eli's. "Not now," she whispered.

Then Scotty appeared at the top of the stairs, backpack in hand, his hair rumpled as usual. "Who's that?"

Gena watched as Scotty sized up the big man standing near the stairs and she also watched Eli's face transform from a scowling mask of restraint and resolve to a genuine smile of curiosity and awe. And she saw a sudden solid terror in those usually fearless eyes, too.

"This is—"

"I'm Eli Trudeau," Eli said, lifting a hand toward Scotty, his voice verging on shaky. "I'm a…friend…your Uncle Devon knows me."

Scotty dropped his backpack and raced down the stairs. "Did you know he's marrying Miss Lydia? I love Miss Lydia. She sends me things—books, CDs, candy. She's so funny. Have you heard her accent? She talks slow 'cause she's from Georgia. I'm gonna be in their wedding."

Gena watched Eli's face light up. Wow, the man could

be a real lady-killer if he worked at it. Shaking that notion right out of her head, she concentrated instead on trying to decide how to explain Eli's presence to her son. "Scotty, aren't you forgetting your manners? Can't you say hello at least."

"Hello," Scotty said, looking sheepish and shy. Then, "*Do* you know Miss Lydia?"

Eli bent down to eye level with Scotty, then reached out to give him a robust handshake. "Nice to finally meet you, Scotty," he said, with emphasis on the finally. "I sure do know Miss Lydia. She is the nicest, kindest, most caring person I've ever met."

Gena could tell Eli actually meant those words and that gave her a sense of hope for his bruised soul.

"She's fun, is all I know," Scotty said with a shrug. "Are you from Georgia? 'Cause you sound funny like Miss Lydia."

Eli stood as Scotty rushed by, headed for the kitchen. Then he called, "I'm from Louisiana. Way down south."

Gena inclined her head. "Better hurry if you want pancakes."

Eli nodded, then held her arm, his head down as he spoke in a soft whisper. "He's so…incredible."

"I know," she said, tears piercing her eyes. "That's why I need you to give me some time."

Eli put his hands in the pocket of his jeans, then lifted his chin toward the kitchen. "I've got lots of time. All the time in the world. And I plan on using it to get to know my son." He stood still for a minute, his gaze moving over her face, then back toward the other room. "But not right now. I can't…not right now."

Then he turned and rushed out the front door. For a minute, Gena couldn't move. She felt trapped between the duty of protecting her son and a mother's love. And she felt trapped by the brilliant shards of happiness and longing she'd seen in Eli's eyes right before the panic and the doubt had taken over. Thinking she should go after him, she started for the door.

Then Scotty called out to her. "Mom, I can't find the syrup." The phone rang, its shrill tone reminding her that she had a job to do and a son to take care of. No time to feel sorry for the man who'd come here to mess with her life.

Gena stared at the door, then turned to go and help her son, grabbing the cordless phone as she moved through the house.

Eli stood out on the craggy rocks, facing the brisk wind coming in off the gray, churning waters of the Atlantic. He was cold, a gentle shiver moving up and down his body. But the shiver wasn't from the frigid air hitting his wet face. It was from a dark fear battering his soul.

Wiping at his eyes, he whispered to the wind. "I'm not good enough for that boy, Lord. Not nearly good enough to even lay claim to him."

He closed his eyes, reliving those precious moments when his son had come down the stairs. Eli's heart had pounded with pride and awe even while it pumped with trepidation.

"Help me," he whispered, his words disappearing as the wind carried them out to sea.

Lydia had told him to turn to God when he was afraid or when he thought he might want to seek revenge or retribution. But there was no retribution here. No way to make up for the losses that boy and he had suffered. Scotty would never know his mother's beautiful smile even though he had the same smile. He'd never hear her pretty Southern drawl. He'd never be able to hug her close and call her "Mommy." And Eli would never have her in his arms again. Never. But he had his son now. If he could face the tremendous responsibility of that.

"Help me."

That was the only prayer his trembling lips could form. So he just stood there, frozen and unyielding, staring out at that harsh, brutal water, tears falling like melting snow-flakes down his face.

Until he felt a hand on his arm.

"Eli, come inside and let me make you some coffee."

He jerked away, then turned to stare at Gena. Her dark hair lifted around her face, her eyes were wide with worry. She clutched his arm, her expression full of a sympathy that just about did him in.

"I'm afraid," he admitted. "I'm so afraid of him."

Gena moved closer. "He's just a little boy. But it is scary, being a parent. It's the kind of love that holds your heart so tightly...well...it's just hard to imagine life without your child."

He turned to her then, understanding piercing the cold wall of his heart. "I came here not knowing, not thinking about that. But now I get it. Fools rush in—"

"Where angels fear to tread," Gena finished.

He touched her hand on his arm, his fingers covering hers. "I'm sorry. So sorry."

Then he saw the tears forming in her eyes. "It's okay. You have a right to know your child. I only ask that you be patient with us. And we'll try to do the same with you."

He faced the ocean again. "I'm normally not a patient man."

"I can tell," she said, her smile indulgent. "Your son has inherited that particular trait, I think."

That made him smile. "I pray he hasn't inherited my other bad traits."

"Time will tell, won't it?"

She shivered as the wind picked up.

"Let's get you inside," he said, turning to take her by the hand.

She nodded, following him back up the slope to the house. "I have scrapbooks—it's a hobby of mine. You're welcome to look at them. They show our life—from the time Devon brought him to me until now."

Eli swallowed back the lump in his throat. "I'd like that."

"C'mon in, then. I'll brew some fresh coffee and I have some homemade cinnamon rolls. You can take as long as you need."

Eli followed her up onto the tiny back porch. He needed a lifetime. But for now, he'd take all the precious moments he could get.

It took a few days, but Eli fell into a routine. He didn't sleep much, but he got up with the sunrise each day to stare over at the cottage across from his own, waiting and sipping coffee until he saw the kitchen light flick on. Then he'd head over to have breakfast with Gena and Scotty, sitting silent and watchful as he absorbed their endearing daily rituals.

After they took Scotty to school, Gena would go about her computer work while Eli would go back to his cottage to look over yet another frilly scrapbook full of pictures of Scotty and Gena.

And what a pretty picture those two made.

Gena decorated each page with cute little captions and colorful cutouts. There were a lot of firsts in those decorative little story boards—first birthday, first Christmas, first tooth, first snowman, first hockey practice. He had missed a lot in the last few years, but these clever picture books told the story of his son's life. Gena loved Scotty, that was for sure.

And so did Eli.

Now as he trudged through the snow to the cottage, he did a visual surveillance—this, too, had become part of his daily routine. So far, nothing seemed amiss even though Eli still woke in the night with a sense of dread in his soul. But he did notice an SUV parked at the cottage across the way on the other side of Gena's house. She'd told him a couple was coming to stay through Christmas. Eli wondered who they were and why they'd chosen such a cold, isolated place to have a vacation. Maybe they wanted some alone time.

He didn't have time to ponder that. His thoughts went back to his son. How did you protect someone when you didn't know what you were trying to protect him or her from?

He couldn't answer his own question. The minute he entered the back door, Scotty bombarded him with fast-paced conversation.

"It's the last day of school, then we get out for the Christmas break," Scotty told Eli in between bites of fluffy pancakes. "Hey, want to help me build a snowman when I get home today, Mr. Eli?"

"I think I'd like that," Eli said, wondering how Gena kept up with this little bundle of energy. He always had another adventure to share. "I've never built a snowman before."

"Honest?" Scotty gave him a look of disbelief. "Why not?"

"Well, we don't get much snow down in Louisiana."

"I'm learning my states," Scotty said, moving on to another subject. "But where's Lous-anna?"

"It's Louisiana," Gena corrected from her spot in front of the stove.

Eli gave Scotty an indulgent smile. He'd been careful not to give out information unless the kid asked. "It's near Texas and the southern part is right on the Gulf of Mexico. That's where I grew up."

"That's big water," Scotty said with a bob of his head.

Eli watched as the kid's hair bounced and bobbed, too. "It is big water, very big. I go shrimpin' in the Gulf a lot whenever I'm home."

"You don't stay home much?"

Eli shook his head. "No, not much. I've been away a long time now. But I might go back soon."

"Maybe one day I can come and visit you," Scotty said on a pragmatic note. "In the summer."

Gena shot Eli a warning look tinged with fear. Although she seemed to trust him more and more each day, Eli wasn't fooled. She was still afraid he'd steal her son away in the middle of the night.

"It gets real hot in Louisiana in the summer," Eli replied, ever careful with his choice of answers. "But you'd be welcome at my door anytime, for sure."

"I could help you catch shrimp."

Eli nodded. "My *maman* used to say '*Les petites mains fait bien avec les petits ouvrages.*' Little hands do well with little tasks."

Scotty giggled. "You talk funny."

Gena placed another batch of pancakes on the table, then sat down. "Eli is Cajun, Scotty, so he's speaking

French. His ancestors left Nova Scotia, Canada, and went all the way to Louisiana many years ago."

"From one big ocean to another one," Eli said, his eyes meeting Gena's. "But that's a long story."

"Cool," Scotty said, draining his milk. "I know where Canada is. We're near there."

"For sure," Eli replied. "One day, I'll tell you all about my Cajun ancestors. People get the wrong impression about us, so I like to set the record straight." He gave Gena a long hard look on that note, hoping she'd try to change her impressions of him. Not that he was making it easy on her. But he had tried to back off and play nice.

Scotty looked confused. "Whatcha talking about?"

"I like to tell people about my culture—the good and bad of it," Eli explained. "It's not all about wrestling 'gators and talking funny, although I do both." He winked, then grinned. "Never met a 'gator I couldn't wrestle."

Scotty's dark eye grew wide. "Have you wrestled a really big one?"

"Not more than six feet or so."

Scotty's gaze filled with wonder. "Wow."

Gena put her hand under her chin and gave him a skeptical look. "I didn't peg you for being so open, Eli. Or so modest." Her sarcasm was cute and he was getting used to this friendly banter even if it was mostly for his son's benefit.

He leaned close, pasting on his best charming smile. "Well, maybe you had me pegged all wrong, *oui?*"

Scotty looked from his mother to Eli. "How'd you guys meet?"

"By accident," Eli said, seamless and simple.

"How long you gonna stay?"

Eli gave Gena a determined stare. "Well, now, that depends on a whole lot of things."

Scotty sat still for a minute. "What do you do, Mr. Eli? For work?"

Gena's head came up and the gloves came off as she stared daggers of warning at him. She'd made it clear in their conversations that she did not want her son involved in CHAIM in any way. And Eli couldn't blame her.

"I do all kinds of things to make a living," Eli said, careful to choose the right words. "I travel a lot and help people in trouble."

"Are we in trouble? I mean you've stayed with us longer than most of our other visitors."

Gena stood and took Scotty's empty plate. "No, we're not in trouble, but you will be if you're late for school. Go brush your teeth and get your coat."

Scotty got up but stopped in front of Eli. "Are you riding to school with us again?"

"I just might," Eli said. "If it's okay with your mom." He'd already insisted it be okay. He'd made it his business to help get Scotty to school and home each day since that first morning. His fear of trouble had easily overcome his fear of being a father. Or at least, he kept telling himself that.

Gena shrugged. "You've been with us every day this week and today is the last day. Why break tradition?"

Eli gave her an appreciative nod, hoping that would cover his real motives.

Scotty pumped his fist. "Will you be here when I get home? To help me with the snowman, remember?"

Eli swallowed, glanced across at Gena. "I'll be right here."

Then he watched as Scotty left the room. *"Mon petit garçon,"* he said, shaking his head. "My little boy."

Gena turned away to stare out the big window behind the sink. Eli could see the ocean churning off in the distance beyond her. He felt that same intense churning inside his stomach.

"What are we going to do, Eli? We can't just stay here in limbo forever."

He got up and came to her, his hand tentative on her arm. "I won't do anything…to upset him. I understand that now. I can't do anything to hurt him. I wouldn't."

She turned, her eyes misty and big and searching. "You've been great these last few days, but are you sure about that?"

Like ice in the sun, his bitter heart melted just a fraction more. "Very sure. I'm not so cold and uncaring that I'd hurt a child…or his mother either, for that matter." He looked down at his boots. "And I told you, I'm sorry about…scaring you that first night. I haven't exactly been trained in the social graces and, funny, there's nothing in the rule books about how to handle finding out you're a father."

"Good, because I can't let you stay here and get close to him if it means he'll be hurt or confused in any way. And I can't—I won't—let you take him away from me. *That* would hurt me. *That* would destroy me."

"Then we have a big problem," he said as he backed away. "I have a legal right to him, but you are his true mother and I can't do that—separate a child from his mother. We're at an impasse, *chère*."

"Yes, we are, but we'll talk about it later." She whirled past him. "I have to take him to school and then I have to make sure our young couple got settled in yesterday."

"You're not taking him to school without me," Eli reminded her, grabbing his coat. Even though he and Gena had reached a truce, he wasn't letting them out of his sight again. Protecting both of them had become his new mission and that meant watching over them for as long as Gena would allow him to do so.

Because he just couldn't shake the feeling that something wasn't right.

FOUR

After watching Gena drop Scotty off at the door and noting a teacher was right there to escort the younger children straight into the building, Eli turned to her. "Is this school secure?"

She kept her gaze on the road. "We've had this conversation already. I told you Devon made sure of that. Besides, they have a resource officer on duty during school hours and at all after-school events."

Eli didn't know why he felt so uneasy this morning. Probably just his lack of sleep and the memories that kept creeping up on him in the dark of night. "Maybe I need to make sure of that myself, just in case."

Gena stopped at a traffic light, then glanced over at him. The brilliant white of the morning snow reflected all around them. "Is there something you're not telling me? You've been jumpy and on high alert since you arrived at my door and even though I know that comes with the territory, you're making me nervous."

He looked out over the snow-covered cottages. Should he tell her? He'd never been one for sharing a lot of information and he really didn't trust anyone. Ever.

But this woman had raised his son and after spending

time with her, Eli could tell she was honest and hardwork-
ing and she took good care of Scotty. Maybe he needed to
bend the rules for her. So she'd understand. "I'm worried
about his safety," he admitted. "I had a long stay in New
Orleans with Kissie after I was released from the hospital.
You know her—the Woman at the Well."

"Devon speaks highly of her. What did she tell you?"

"We had some information come through. Might be
nothing, might be something."

She hit the steering wheel with her palms. "And you
waited almost a week to mention this? You'd better tell me
everything, and I mean everything."

He touched a hand to the dash. "After you get me home.
I hate snow and ice."

Gena's hands were shaking so hard, she couldn't unlock
the door. "So this is the real reason you came all the way
up here. You're worried about Scotty, right?"

Eli grabbed the keys from her, then jammed them into the
lock. Pushing her in out of the cold, he turned and handed
her the keys, then reset the alarm. "That's part of it, true. After
the dust settled on my grandfather's criminal deeds, Kissie
and Devon assured me that everything was all right, but they
couldn't get verification on some of his associates. People
who were involved with my grandfather were making inquiries about things they didn't need to know, and that's all we
could find out—not the who or the why. I need facts and I
like details. Not being one to wait around, I wanted to see for
myself that Scotty was truly safe." He shrugged off his coat.
"And I've been watching all week to make sure. So far, things
seem okay, but I just can't seem to shake this feeling. I don't
like taking other people's word for things, you understand?"

"I'm beginning to understand a lot," she retorted, as she stalked up the hall. "You came here to see Scotty and you've also been casing my house, haven't you? I suppose you've tested every lock, checked and rechecked the security and memorized every way off this peninsula just to be sure. But you need to tell me the whole story. I have a right to know. You've just been twiddling your thumbs, sitting around when—" She froze as she came to her desk tucked into an alcove just off the kitchen.

Eli saw her halt, heard her intake of breath, and the hair on the back of his neck stood straight up. "What is it?"

"My laptop is on." She dropped her tote bag and hurried to the tidy desk. "And my papers have been rearranged."

Eli looked at the efficient little desk. He'd walked by it enough to know something wasn't quite right. Gena was tidy to the point of being obsessive and she always closed her laptop whenever she wasn't using it. He'd seen her do that several times.

"Are you sure you didn't leave it open before we left?"

She stood staring at it, then breathed a sigh of relief. "You know, I think I might have. Remember, I had that couple coming to check in? They're renting the other cabin through Christmas."

"But that was last night, right?"

She nodded, touched a hand to the papers on her desk. "But the man called this morning and had some questions about their bill. I pulled up the account, then looked through the papers on my desk to give him a local restaurant number." She whirled, shaking her head. "Then Scotty couldn't find one of his school books, so I rushed to help him. I guess I left everything in a mess as we hurried out the door."

Eli remembered that much at least. She'd called to

Scotty that they were going to be late. He tried to let it go at that. But…he'd never been one to accept things on a surface level. Because by his way of thinking, things were never what they seemed.

"What did your guest—Bennett's the name, right—what did Mr. Bennett ask you?"

"He just asked about an extra charge on their deposit. I explained about the linen service. Then he asked me about where to get a good Maine breakfast. I told him about the café up the road. We made small talk about the weather, then he hung up."

"Are you sure?"

She gave him a puzzled look. "Yes, pretty sure. You don't think—?"

"I need to know for certain," he said, turning at the door. "I'm gonna walk the perimeters of your property. See what's what."

Gena halted him with her hand on his arm. "Eli, are you being *completely* honest with me? You can't come here and do this. I mean, you can't just put yourself in charge like some guardian or bodyguard, based on a bad feeling. I don't mind you wanting to see Scotty, but if you know something…" She inhaled a deep breath. "I couldn't bear it if something happens to him."

Eli saw the fear in her eyes and hated it. He'd known that same fear and he lived it over and over in his nightmares. He hadn't been able to save Leah and he hadn't been around to help Gena raise Scotty. Maybe he was just imagining things and scaring her unnecessarily because he needed to prove something to himself. Turning back to face her, he said, "Look, I'm just a paranoid kind of guy. I've been trained to be that way. So don't let me worry you. I always take extra precautions. Even more now that—"

Understanding dawned in her eyes. "Now that you've lost your wife and never knew your son?"

"Isn't that reason enough?" he asked, hoping she'd see the sincerity in his eyes. "I've got a lot of ground to cover."

He opened the door and felt the arctic blast of winter hitting him in the face and he knew in his heart he'd walk the whole earth if need to be. To protect his son.

And Gena, too.

Gena fidgeted around her desk, searching for any signs of sabotage or espionage. She didn't like this. Since the day Devon had brought Scotty to her, she'd had to watch her back. Caution had become second nature to her, but only because she always knew that one day *he'd* show up. Eli Trudeau was not the kind of man to ignore his own flesh and blood, especially when that flesh and blood had been taken from him without his consent.

But that was the least of her worries today. Eli was here now and as much as she feared the worst, she knew he'd do what was best for Scotty. He was that kind of man.

No, today her caution and concern centered on the other dangers out there, dangers that Eli might have stirred by showing up here. What was Eli hiding? Did he know something horrible that he refused to tell her? Or was he truly just being overprotective?

She went to the window to look for him. He wasn't in the front yard. Hurrying to the back of the house, she looked out toward the sea and saw him standing on one of the craggy bluffs, staring out at the constantly crashing ocean. That seemed to be part of his daily routine now.

Gena immediately put on her coat and rushed out the back door toward him. "Eli?"

He turned when he heard her voice. "I talked to Devon," he said, a frown marring his face. "He ripped me up one side and down another for being here in the first place, but he's going to check into things for us."

She inched closer, pulling the fur of her coat collar up around her face. "What kind of things?"

"We'll start with your computer. Since he's set up to monitor all your files anyway, he'll do a complete scan to see if it's been compromised."

"He does that routinely. How can that help?"

"Well, now, he'll do an extra check just for good measure. Devon knows ways to find out things no one would think to look for and it'll be much more discreet for him to do it from a long-distance location." He glanced toward where the car he'd seen earlier was still parked at the other cottage. "Looks like your boarders are settled in and back from breakfast."

Gena glanced around. "I hadn't even noticed. I left them a key at the door. They weren't sure when they'd get here."

"Well, they must have come in the middle of the night." He gave her a direct stare. "We'll need to do a more in-depth background check on them, too."

Gena couldn't believe this. "They're just a young couple from New York."

"And they drove up to Maine because?"

"That's their business."

"Criminals come in all shapes and sizes, Gena."

She couldn't read his expression. "Is there more here?"

He shook his head. "Not for now. We'll just have to watch and wait."

"Easy for you to say. It's close to Christmas, Eli, and tomorrow is Scotty's birthday and the Christmas play at the church. How can I relax when I'm so worried?"

He turned to her, his skin flushed from the cold, his dark hair swirling around his face and neck. He had the blackest eyes, unreadable and bottomless, sometimes cold and calculating, sometimes warm and liquid. "Let's keep things cool for Scotty's sake, okay? You'll get your postcard-perfect Christmas." He turned toward the house.

"I don't want a perfect Christmas. I want a safe one. I want my son safe. Can you promise me that?"

He stopped, looking at her with such intensity that Gena took a step back. "That's why I'm here. We can agree on that, at least."

It was Christmas Eve. Scotty's birthday—or rather, the day Gena celebrated his birthday.

Eli trudged across the snow toward the warmth of Gena's cottage, his gaze encompassing the yard and woods as a frigid dusk settled over the land. The snowman Scotty and he had built stood fat and formidable, wearing a black muffler and an old battered baseball cap. Noting the young couple's car was gone from next door, he wondered when he'd hear anything back from Kissie on their background. On the surface, Craig and Marcy Bennett looked as all-American and squeaky clean as a toothpaste ad. They took long walks along the bluffs, holding hands and cooing sweet nothings in each other's ears and they waved to Eli in passing. Mostly they kept to themselves. Perfectly normal activities for a young married couple in love.

Too perfect. Too normal. Eli didn't like the perfection of it all.

"You're scowling," Gena said as he opened the door and entered the kitchen, rubbing his hands together as the heat hit him.

"I hate snow and cold," he retorted to hide his concerns.

"We all get that, Eli," she replied with a wry smile. "Can't you fake it for Scotty's sake at least?" She pointed to the cake she'd baked earlier. "It's a celebration. But first we're off to the Christmas Eve play at church."

Eli took in the "Happy Birthday, Scotty" lettering on the big cake. "I thought I'd skip the play."

"You have to go, Mr. Eli," Scotty said from his spot at the arched doorway. "I'm playing a sheep."

Eli looked from Gena to his son. "I didn't see you there, *petit peu.*"

Gena shot Eli a daring glance. "We'd like you to go to church with us tonight."

Eli knew a feminine command when he heard one. And how could he refuse either of them? "Okay, then. I guess that particular problem is settled. I'll be on my best behavior, sitting in the very front pew."

Scotty giggled. "You'll see me up close in my sheep costume. Mama made it and it tickles our noses."

Eli touched a finger to Scotty's nose, giving it his own tickle. "Do you get to go 'Baahhh'?"

Another giggle. "Nope. I just stand there, watching over Baby Jesus."

"And you sing songs to praise Him," Gena reminded him.

"That's right." Scotty rushed to the table. "Wow, chocolate cake. My favorite." Turning to Eli, he held up his fingers. "I'm six today."

"Hard to imagine," Eli said, sinking down in a chair as his legs became weak. This kind of love could do that to a man: bring him to his knees. "You're growing up right before my eyes."

"Silly," Scotty said with a shrug. "You only just got here a few days ago. But when Mom got me, I was a tiny baby—like Jesus."

Eli ran a hand down his face. "I wish I could have seen you then." He glanced up at Gena, saw the sympathy in her eyes and pulled out his pent-up rage to counter it. Shutting his eyes, he willed the rage back down and willed her to stop feeling sorry for him. When he opened his eyes, she was still watching him. But she didn't say anything.

"When can I have cake?" Scotty asked, innocent to the rippling undercurrents in the cinnamon-scented room.

"After church." Gena replied. "We'll come back here and let you open your birthday present."

"I get one big present for my birthday and then a couple for Christmas, too," Scotty explained to Eli. "I hope the big one is my new skates and a hockey stick."

Pushing past the lump in his throat, Eli said, "That's more than one present, isn't it?"

Scotty bobbed his head. "Yes, sir, but they kinda go together, so Mom said she might get me both."

"I see." Eli smiled over at Scotty, content to bask in the warmth of his son's sweet innocence. He wondered if this is how his mother had felt when he was young and innocent. He wondered how many times she'd cried herself to sleep when he'd gone from good to bad and never looked back. He'd joined CHAIM, thinking his deceased father would have been proud of him. Thinking his wealthy, powerful grandfather might notice him. Well, that hadn't gone very well, had it, since the man had tried to kill him.

I won't let that happen to you, he thought now as he watched Scotty eat his peanut-butter-and-jelly sandwich. I won't let you grow up without me, without knowing how proud I am of you. Eli had bought the boy some gifts, but that wouldn't nearly cover all that he'd missed. "And what did you ask for for Christmas?"

"That's easy," Scotty said after he drained his milk. He looked right into Eli's eyes and said, "I just wish my daddy would come to see me. That's what I'd really like. Mama said he might come back one day. Wouldn't it be cool if he came on Christmas?"

Eli heard Gena's gasp of surprise. He looked from his son to her, his heart splitting into jagged pieces. He'd been stabbed, shot at, even tortured at times, but he'd never felt such an intense pain. It floored him and made him want to scream out for relief.

"Scotty, you need to go up and wash your face," Gena said, her words low and hollow. "I'll be up to help you put on your costume in a few minutes."

"But Mom—"

"Go on. We can't be late for the play."

She managed to push him toward the door, then watched as he hurried up the stairs. Then she found the nearest chair and collapsed down beside Eli, her eyes closed, her hands covering her face.

"He's smart," Eli said in a stunned whisper. "He's going to figure this out."

"It's so hard," she whispered, her eyes still closed. "How do we explain?"

Eli wanted to reach out to her, but his guilt and his shame held him back. "I have no idea," he said.

Then he saw her lips moving and knew she was praying—

for all of them. Eli took her hand, letting her pray. Maybe God would hear her gentle pleas and maybe, somehow by God's grace, Scotty would get his Christmas wish.

FIVE

The church was pristine and quaint, a small stone and wood chapel with a rising bell steeple sitting in the heart of the little village proper about three miles from the turnoff to Gena's house. Captive Cove wasn't a big place. Eli had noted the population sign that boasted three hundred and three citizens when he'd first rode to school with Gena and Scotty. But tonight, it looked as if all of those citizens had come to the Christmas play.

He hated crowds.

"I'm going to sit by the back door," he said to Gena under his breath as they left the cold and entered the toasty warm entryway. He was already breaking a sweat.

"You told Scotty you'd be right up front," she countered, frowning. "He'll wonder where you are."

"Is there an exit up there?"

She nodded, then let out a sigh. "Yes, of course. You're worse than Dev about such things. Are you all right?"

"What do you think? I hate crowds and my son is about to be on stage. I'm not used to this, Gena."

He hated the soft smile on her pretty lips. "The fearless Eli Trudeau is afraid of a little boy playing a sheep?"

"Do not tease me," he said in a low growl. "That's not very nice."

"I'm not teasing you. I'm trying to make you relax. You'll be fine, Eli. Just sit back and enjoy the play. It's really cute. And we're safe here, at least."

"For sure. I hate cute, too." And he wasn't so sure about being safe. It was a sanctuary, he told himself. Lydia would tell him he was safe in God's house. Sometimes, Eli thought he'd never feel safe again.

"Do you have any social graces at all?" Gena asked, snapping him out of his concerns.

He wanted to tell her that he'd never been trained in anything but survival, but he refrained. "*Non*, not a one. I was raised on the bayou, remember. My *maman* let me run wild. And I'm still wild."

"I believe that," Gena said as she pushed him down on a cold steel folding chair near a little hallway. "Sit."

"Yes, ma'am," he retorted with a salute. "Is it hot in here to you?"

"It's warm. But I thought you'd like that."

"I hate ice and snow, but I don't like to sweat either."

"I didn't think you did sweat. You've kept your cool through everything but having to face your son."

Eli pushed at his hair, then tugged off his heavy pea coat. "Well, he's hard to face. I don't like lying to him."

That took the pretty smile right off her face. "We're protecting him until I can explain."

Eli nodded. "How long does this play last?"

Gena slapped his hand. "Honestly, just relax. Being a parent means you get to sit through a lot of plays and programs and school events." She stopped, her eyes holding his. "I'm sorry. I know it's not easy."

Eli decided to stop being a big baby. He had to be courageous for his son's sake, didn't he? "I'm okay. Just nervous. What if he falls off the stage or something?"

"He won't. He only has to stand there and sing."

"Okay. I think I can deal with that." He turned to scope the crowd. "Do you know all of these people?"

Gena nodded. "I know most of them. This is a very tight-knit community."

"And you can vouch for them?"

"Yes, I can. The salt of the earth—that's what they are." As if to prove that, she turned and greeted an older couple right behind them, then introduced them to Eli. "He's a friend of Devon," she explained. "Just passing through. He's staying in one of my cottages."

"Nice to meet you," the woman said, giving Eli a wide smile. "It's good to know Gena and Scotty have company for Christmas."

"Good to be here," Eli said in a strained breath.

Thankfully, the lights went down and the play's diminutive director, a woman named Irene, came out onto the stage to give an overview of the whole thing. Eli didn't have to make small talk anymore. He glanced over his shoulder one more time, then gave Gena a tight smile.

Gena stared over at him. "I am glad you're here," she said on a whisper. "You make *me* feel safe."

Eli's heart turned as soft as fleece. He glanced around, hoping no one had heard that comment. Then he caught a glance of a man standing in the back of the church. Was that Craig Bennett?

"Did you invite our neighbors to come?" he asked Gena, his mind on full alert.

"I mentioned it when I saw them outside earlier today, yes."

Before Eli could tell her he thought they were here, a host of tiny angels began singing in unison up on the stage and from that moment on, he was entertained and enthralled enough to forget all about Craig Bennett.

"Thanks, Mom."

Scotty beamed as he held his brand-new hockey stick and then dropped to the floor to examine his new skates. "Coach will be glad I've finally got the right equipment."

"Coach doesn't have to worry about broken bones or chipped teeth," Gena countered. "But...I have to admit you're pretty good."

"You ever played hockey, Mr. Eli?"

Eli looked down at Scotty, the lump in his throat growing so strong, he could barely swallow. "No, never." He didn't tell his son that he'd used a couple of hockey sticks before to hurt bad guys. Scotty didn't need to hear the details of that. "I reckon you'll have to show me a few moves tomorrow...if it's okay with your mama."

"We got a pond down the lane," Scotty said, grabbing the stick to demonstrate. "It's frozen solid. That's where I practice." Then he whirled to Gena. "Want to come and watch us, Mom?"

"I just might," Gena said. "We'll need some exercise after our big Christmas dinner."

"She cooks ham and turkey and all kinds of vegetables," Scotty said, making a face. "I have to eat some broccoli before I can have cake."

"What a mighty challenge," Eli replied. "What kind of cake?"

"Apple and walnut," Scotty replied. "And we have birthday cake."

"I might eat my vegetables, too, for some of that."

Gena shook her head and headed to the kitchen. "Speaking of, I did promise birthday cake after church. I'll make some coffee for us," she said to Eli.

"I want milk with mine," Scotty replied, admiring his presents.

Eli pulled out a wrapped box. "Here's one from me. Happy Birthday, Scotty." Proud that he'd managed to say that without breaking into tears, Eli leaned back on the comfortable sofa to watch his son. A man sure could get used to this. It was nice here in this little cottage, with the fire burning and the smells of chocolate and coffee wafting through the air. It was nice to have a son...and a woman who loved that son.

He sat there and wondered when he'd need to come out of this lovely limbo. And if he'd ever be able to leave his son behind.

Scotty's shout of glee brought Gena back into the den. "What is it?"

"It's an LSU football," Scotty said, throwing it toward Eli without warning. "Mr. Eli says they're playing a big game after Christmas."

"Down in the Superdome," Eli replied, his grin broad.

"Did you go to college at Louisiana State?" Gena asked, wanting to know everything about him. And wondering if he'd brought that football here with him since she was pretty sure he hadn't found it in town.

"I did some community college," he said with a shrug. "Wasn't enough money to finish." At her questioning look, he lifted his brows. "I got my education...through work."

"Ah, yes," she said, nodding. "I forgot. Your *company* makes all of its employees get an education, right?"

"In more ways than one," he said, tossing the football back and forth to Scotty. Then he looked uncomfortable. "Enough for now, Scotty. We don't want to knock over the Christmas tree. Let's go find that cake."

Gena watched as he walked past her with Scotty like a shadow on his heels. Her son would miss Eli after he was gone. And so would she.

They pulled out chairs by the oak dining table, but Gena motioned to Scotty to wash his hands first. Gena could feel Eli's dark eyes on her. She wondered what he thought about her. She knew his wife had been beautiful. Devon had described Leah as being very ethereal and womanly, almost fragile. Gena was anything but fragile. She worked out to stay in shape and she had a hearty appetite. Tonight, she'd dressed in a long black wool skirt over black boots and the cream cashmere sweater with tiny pearls around the neckline that Devon had given her for Christmas last year. Plain and simple and warm. Not ethereal.

And why did she care? she wondered. Eli was here for Scotty, not her. He might leave them in peace or he might insist that his son come to live with him in Louisiana. Either way, Gena's life would never be the same.

When she sat down, he touched a hand to hers. "What's wrong?"

"Wrong?" She shrugged, aware of her son nearby washing his hands. "Nothing. I just hope we can work things out between us."

"We will," he said. Then he leaned close. "You look pretty."

Gena blushed, wondering if the man could read her thoughts. "Thanks. Working at home, I don't dress up much."

"You look pretty not dressed up, too."

The gleam in his eyes made her smile and it also made her shake. "Are you flirting with me, Eli?"

He slanted his head sideways. "Could be."

Gena laughed. "It's been a while...."

"For me, too, *chère*. I only ever knew Leah. She was all I had and I was not easy to love."

Gena looked down at the Christmas place mat that glittered with gold threads slipping through a bright red-and-green plaid. "All I ever knew was Richard. And we had very little time together. It was tough until the night Devon showed up with Scotty."

"Are you guys holding hands?"

Scotty's question broke them apart and shattered the intimacy Gena felt looking into Eli's eyes.

"We need to say grace," she replied, hoping to distract her son. Scotty waited until after she'd said, "Amen," then continued.

"Are you two dating or something?"

Gena looked over at Eli, alarm pumping through her heart. "Of course not. Why would you think that?"

"Mr. Eli is here a lot, is all." He looked over at Eli. "I like him, though."

Eli burst into laughter at that. "For true, I like you, too." Then he cuffed Scotty on the arm. "And I have to admit, I kinda like your mama."

"Then I think you could date her," Scotty replied. "I mean, I don't mind."

"Thanks for your blessings," Eli replied, grinning as he swallowed a big slab of cake.

"Yes, thanks so much." Gena looked down at her plate,

then glanced back up at her son. "Scotty, we're just friends, okay? Don't get your hopes up."

Scotty shook his head, cake crumbs around his mouth. "I'm not hoping, Mom. But I did ask God in my prayers."

After Scotty had reluctantly gone to bed, Gena came back downstairs to find Eli standing by the front window watching the snow fall.

"You can barely hear it," he said, motioning to the whitewashed woods. "Only if you listen real hard."

Gena looked out at the dark woods. "It's like a big cocoon."

"But it's bitter cold out there."

"Then come back by the fire," she said. "Why do you hate the cold so much, anyway, Eli?"

He sat down, facing the blue-tipped flames, his coffee mug clutched in his hands. "I was cold the night they came and told me that someone had taken my wife. And I haven't been really warm since then." He touched his heart. "Not inside, not in here."

Gena couldn't speak. Such a complex man, with the ability to hurt her and the ability to go all soft on her. Her heart ached for the time he'd lost with Scotty after the horrible grief of losing his wife. She knew that kind of deep grief herself.

"I searched for her day and night. I stayed out there, searching, through rain and cold. It was November when the report came in that she might never be found. It was December when they finally located her. But I wasn't around then and they didn't bother finding me. I took off, went down to Grand Isle just to get away. When I came back…and kind of went off the deep end, they shipped me off to Ireland to a CHAIM stronghold—to rest, to get well. And I was cold the whole time I stayed there, cold and trapped and so lonely. I just wish I could have gone to her, talked to her, held her."

Gena leaned close, touching a hand to the soft wool of his sweater. "I'm sorry you had to go through that."

He didn't speak for a while. "My son was born while I was out there just about to lose my mind with worry and grief. I was in no shape to help either of them." Then he looked up at her and she saw the torment in his eyes. "No wonder Devon sent me to the CHAIM retreat in Ireland. I just wish…"

Gena pulled him close, wrapping her arms around his neck. "You're here now. Listen to me. Just close your eyes and listen to me." She felt his resistance at first, then she felt him slump into her embrace. "When Devon brought him to me, he was so tiny but so strong. His hair was dark and curly even as a newborn and his eyes, I think, are a combination of yours and his mother's—sometimes blue, sometimes almost black. I took him in my arms, Eli, and I fell in love. Your son brought me comfort when I thought there was none. He restored my faith in God. He gave me hope. I held him that night and he took my finger in his little fist and he held tight. He held tight to *me*. And I've held tight to him since. I want you to know that I've tried to love him and protect him and…"

She didn't realize she was crying until Eli looked up and touched a finger to her face. And she didn't realize he was crying until he pulled her close and kissed her.

Then Gena felt his tears merging with her own and realized that they'd been destined to find each other and to bring comfort to each other. Their tears for the little boy they both loved had just sealed that fate. And Eli's lips on hers had just sealed what she'd felt in her heart.

She was beginning to have feelings for Scotty's father.

* * *

Hours later, Gena woke to find Eli's hand over her mouth. Frightened that he'd somehow gotten this close without her knowing it, she pushed at him and tried to speak. Had she dreamed that he'd kissed her earlier and held her in his arms? Had she been wrong about trusting him?

Eli loosened his hand but held a finger to her lips. Tugging her up and into the hallway, he looked around then pulled her close. "Don't say anything unless you whisper."

"But—"

He took her face in his hand. "Shh." Then he spelled out in a silent whisper, "B-U-G-S."

Gena twisted away, shock in her eyes. "You can't be serious," she said, her voice low.

He mouthed the words, "Devon called. We've been compromised."

Compromised. Gena knew what that meant. Someone had planted listening devices in her house. Feeling sick with the knowledge of that, she squirmed toward Scotty's room. "Scotty—"

"He's safe," Eli said into her ear, his hand solid on her flannel pajama sleeve as he dragged her downstairs by the glow of a tiny flashlight. He felt the picture frames along the walls, then worked his way toward the computer desk, touching lamps and lifting knickknacks. He didn't make a sound and he kept pointing to her to lift things here and there. Then he jabbed a finger toward the laptop.

Gena put a hand to her mouth, then grabbed a notepad off the desk. She wrote, "Do you think someone messed with my computer?"

Eli took the pen. "Yes." Then he wrote something else on the pad and shoved it at her. "We need to take Scotty and leave. Soon."

Gena couldn't believe what he'd just written. "Leave? What do you mean? I can't leave."

Eli went to the radio and turned it down low on *Here Comes Santa Claus*. Then he pulled her up onto the stairs, sat her down and after scanning the banister with his hands, leaned close in front of her. In a deep whisper, he said, "Devon confirmed it. Someone has compromised both your house and your computer. Devon found a questionable breach after he ran a new security scan on your files today. He thinks someone's been monitoring your software—and possibility your security code for entry into the house."

"A hacker?"

He nodded. "But we're not sure what kind or why."

Gena tried to hide the trembles shooting throughout her system, but Eli steadied her with a hand on each arm. She wanted to run as fast as she could to her son, but she didn't push Eli away. She needed the strength he was offering right now. "My computer has a state-of-the-art debugging system. Devon saw to that. Nothing gets through my files."

He shook his head. "Someone did. Do you know everything there is to know about these corporations you build sites for?"

"As much as possible to do my job." Then she gasped. "You don't think—?"

"I think my number one rule still holds true. Trust no one. You'd be surprised how dangerous people can walk around looking like saints. And how someone who wants to do harm can plant a lunatic amongst sane people."

"You think someone I work for is behind this? Or that they sent someone here?"

"Don't know. Could be."

"Don't go all cryptic on me now, Eli. My son's safety is at stake."

"And your own, *catin.*" He let her go, then sank down beside her. "My first instinct is to go get Scotty and leave. But…I'm learning to be a bit more cool and calm in my old age. I need to think about how to handle this."

Gena liked the first idea better. "I just want Scotty to be okay."

Eli nodded. "Here's what we do, then. I have a secure cell phone that we can use to talk to Devon. I might be able to see if anything has been sabotaged or compromised by looking over your files, but then, I'll have to be really careful. You go get dressed and pack a bag for you and Scotty. Then we'll decide what to do."

She bobbed her head, shocked and dazed. "But…why would someone come to my house to plant a bug? I mean, they could mess with my laptop from anywhere on earth with the right equipment, which they obviously did."

"That's the rub," he said, letting out a sigh. "I think they wanted to get the scope of the house, see what's what. Like…where the boy—where Scotty sleeps."

Gena shot up. "No, no, don't tell me that. Don't tell me that."

She didn't realize she was shouting the words until Eli stood and pulled her into his arms. His big warm body felt like a cocoon or maybe like a swaddling blanket, trapping her inside a net of sheer terror. And because she didn't want to face that terror, she lashed out at him. "You brought this on us. You brought this on *him.*"

The look of disgrace and pain in Eli's eyes shattered her and made her wish she hadn't said those hateful words. "*Oui,* maybe I did at that. Or maybe I got here just in time, *non?*"

"I don't know," she said. "Eli, you have to protect him. Do you understand me?"

Eli tugged her against him. "I understand plenty, *chère,* more than plenty. I won't let any harm come to him, I promise."

"How am I supposed to trust you, when you told me not to trust anyone?"

The next song on the radio was a poignant classic Christmas hymn. "Away in a Manger" filled the house with hope and calm. Eli lifted his hands to Gena's face and made her look him in the eye. "Do you see me? Do you see what I'm telling you here? Look at me, Gena."

Gena saw the sincerity in his gaze, saw the plea for her to believe him. She nodded. "I want to believe you."

He inched closer. "You know I came for my son." He stopped, swallowed, stared at her. "I love the boy. *Il est mon coeur.*"

She knew enough French to interpret that endearing phrase. "He is my heart, too, Eli. Please remember that."

Eli didn't answer her with words. Instead, he held a thumb to her cheek and caught the single tear that fell down her face, reminding her of the bond that had grown between them, reminding her that they both loved Scotty.

"I need you," she said. "Eli, I need you to help me."

"Then you have to do exactly as I say," he whispered. "Go and check on Scotty, then start packing."

Gena turned to go upstairs, but his hand on hers brought

her back around and he kissed her full on the lips. "We're in this together, Gena, understand?"

"Yes," she said, even as a chill of dread moved down her spine.

SIX

Gena tiptoed into Scotty's room. Her son was sleeping, his superhero pajama sleeves shining a bright red and yellow against the thick comforter. She kissed him on the forehead, then turned to find him some clothes. That's when she heard the noise in the corner.

Gena whirled. "Who's there?"

A man stepped out of the shadows. "Just me, Miss Malone."

"Mr. Bennett?" Gena's heart stopped cold. Eli had been right about their neighbors after all. "What are you doing in my son's room?"

Craig Bennett chuckled low, then waved a gun in the air. "Well, now, I'm supposed to be taking the boy with me. But your friend downstairs has seriously interfered with that plan, hasn't he?"

"I don't know what you mean," Gena said, all the while looking for some kind of weapon. Her son wasn't leaving with this man. "I'm alone. I just came in to check on Scotty." Taking a deep breath, she said, "Can you tell me why you'd want to take a little boy away from his mother on Christmas?"

"You don't need to know the details," Craig replied.

"But I'm afraid you will have to be part of the plan now. You should be asleep across the hall. But Eli Trudeau came to the rescue, didn't he? A real menace, that one."

Gena looked out into the dark hallway. "That's an understatement. You don't want to mess with him."

"I don't intend to," Bennett replied, his teeth glistening as he grinned. "I'm leaving that bit of work to my partner, Marcy. She has such a crush on him."

Eli walked along the rocks, talking low into the phone. "Are you sure this service is secure, Dev?"

"Yes," Devon replied. "I've verified it all the way to the top. What's the plan, Eli?"

Eli shrugged, the frigid air taking his breath. "I have to get them away from here. I think the couple that showed up a few days ago might be in on this."

"Their background check came back clean," Devon said.

"*Oui,* but we both know that doesn't mean anything, don't we, *mon ami?*"

He heard Devon's intake of breath. "True. So…don't bother with doing anything to get even with them for now. Just get Scotty and my sister out of there."

"That's the plan," Eli said, thinking his old friend knew him too well. "But this time, I aim to do things by the book. For Scotty's sake. That's why I wanted to clear it with you. You're my witness, Dev."

"I hear you. You have my word on that. I'll vouch for anything you decide. I trust you, Eli."

Eli closed his eyes. "Thanks, bro. Got to go."

"Be careful," Devon warned.

Eli turned around and felt the force of something broad and heavy ramming against his skull. And then the crashing of the ocean warred with the crashing pain inside his head just before he hit the rocks.

"Okay, here's the plan," Craig Bennett said as he shoved Gena toward Scotty's bed. "You and the boy will come with us. Once we deliver Scotty, well, I'm not sure what we'll do with you, but…I get paid to keep my mouth shut. So…"

"So you're going to take my son and kill me?" Gena asked, her gaze hitting on Scotty's hockey stick leaning against his nightstand.

"Can't answer that. This is a no-questions-asked assignment."

"Who sent you?"

"Can't tell you. Then I'd have to kill you." He laughed at his own wit. "Now, get the boy up and get some clothes on him. Dress him warm. It's cold outside."

Gena heard footsteps on the stairs—Eli, she hoped. The noise was just enough of a distraction to cause Craig to turn. Just enough of a distraction to give her a chance to grab the hockey stick. She brought it up and with all her strength, swung it around toward Craig Bennett's head and gave him a hard whack. He went down with a groan. Scotty sat up in bed, calling out to Gena. As she turned to her son, she felt a poke in her ribs.

"Don't move."

It wasn't Eli. Marcy was holding the gun this time.

Eli woke with a start. A cold spray of ocean water blasted him in the face, bringing him fully alert. He rolled over and up, dizzy and disoriented. Then he remembered. Gena and Scotty were in trouble.

Eli took off toward the dark cottage, his heart pounding

with his throbbing head. He didn't have a weapon. Searching for anything, he found an old piece of driftwood lying by the back door and grabbed it as he hurried inside the house. He hit the stairs when he heard a scream and a thump coming from Scotty's room.

"Gena?" Eli took the stairs in record time. "Gena, are you all right?"

"In here," he heard her call.

Eli entered the room, the piece of wood held high in the air. Then he looked down at the two people on the floor. Relief washed over him. "I see you put your self-defense training to good use, *chère*."

"They were trying to hurt Mom," Scotty said, rushing to Eli. "I hit the woman after Mom took down that mean man."

Gena was shaking as she fell against Eli. "I used the hockey stick on him and Scotty hit her with one of his skates."

"We need to get out of here," Eli said. He shot Gena a meaningful look. "Take Scotty and grab what you can. I have to take care of a few things. I'll meet you downstairs."

"Are they dead?" Scotty asked as Gena pushed him toward the door.

"No," Eli replied. He hated subjecting his son to this kind of violence. "Just hurt. Go with your mama."

He watched them leave, then went to work searching for something to tie up the couple. The blind cords would have to do. Taking out his knife, he quickly clipped four cords long enough to do the job. In a few minutes, he had both of them tied up against the closet door.

The man came to long enough to moan and stare up at Eli. Eli took Craig Bennett's face in his hand. "You have made a grave mistake, my friend. You tried to harm someone I love."

Craig moaned and used an expletive Eli couldn't repeat.

"Who sent you?" Eli asked. "And don't make me force it out of you."

"Can't tell you," Craig said on a hiss of breath.

Eli leaned close. "I don't have time to play games, so here's the deal. I'm taking Scotty and Gena and I'm leaving. You will stay tied up here until someone comes for you, understand?"

Bennett's eyes showed panic. "You didn't call the cops, did you?"

Eli heard the fear in the man's question. "No, I'm a nice person. Wouldn't do that. We don't need to involve the cops, now do we?"

"No," Craig replied, shutting his eyes to what must be the lingering pain of being hit with a hockey stick.

"I thought you'd agree. I'm going to call one of my superiors to send help. By the time you wake up again, you'll be a long way from here."

"I'm not planning on passing out again," Craig said. "And I can get out of these blind cords easily."

"I know that," Eli said with a smile. "That's why I have to do this."

He knocked Craig out cold, checked his pulse, then turned to Marcy. She was alive but she had a deep gash on her temple. Probably have a concussion at least. CHAIM would take care of their injuries and hold them until they talked. That was all Eli could deal with right now. He dialed Devon again. "We're leaving." He explained the situation. "Find the nearest agent to come and clean up this mess," he told his friend. "We'll be long gone by the time they arrive."

Devon promised reinforcements. "Eli, take care of them."

"You know I will." He gathered up Scotty's hockey stick and his skates. They might come in handy again.

"Where are you taking them?"

"Better you don't know that, *mon ami.*"

He clicked the phone shut before Devon could protest. He might be doing things by the book these days, but that didn't mean he had to share anything with anyone.

Trust no one.

Right now, that was the best plan of action.

"But what about Santa?"

Eli looked over his shoulder at Scotty. The boy was all tucked in his seat belt in the small back seat of Eli's truck.

Trying to calm his son, Eli replied, "Funny thing about that. Santa left your presents right there under the tree. You can open them when we come back home."

Gena shot him an appreciative look. "Thank you."

Scotty leaned forward, straining against his seat belt. "Where are you taking us? Did Santa see those mean people? Why did they break into our house?"

Eli clutched the steering wheel, careful to take it slow on the winding, icy road to the main highway. "You sure ask a lot of questions, but I'll do my best to answer them. We're going somewhere safe so I can take care of you and your mama. Santa didn't see the bad guys, but I'll make sure he puts them both on his naughty list for a very long time. And they probably broke into your house because they don't have the love of Christ in their hearts and they only know how to do horrible things."

Gena sent him another look. Eli shrugged. "I'm trying to think like my friend Lydia, okay?"

"You're doing fine," she said, but he saw the shadows in her eyes.

"Try not to worry," he told her. Then he glanced in the rearview mirror at Scotty. "Get some sleep, Scotty."

Scotty looked back at him, his gaze solemn. "Did my Uncle Devon send you here to take care of us, Mr. Eli?"

Eli's hand tightened on the steering wheel. "No, he didn't, but he asked me to do that very thing. And I will. You have my word on that."

Scotty bobbed his head, then shut his eyes. In a few minutes, he was fast asleep, his head slumping against the seat.

Gena turned to check on her son, then faced Eli. "What's going on? And I want the whole story, Eli. Somebody tried to take my son tonight and I want to know why."

He didn't bother answering her right away. Instead, he remained silent and watchful until they were past Penobscot Bay and heading south on Highway 1.

"Where are we going, Eli?" Gena asked again, hoping he would open up to her. She knew he was trying to protect her, but Gena was used to dealing with things on her own. That wouldn't change now. Especially now.

"We're going south," he replied in a cryptic tone.

"I can see that," she retorted. "Don't insult my intelligence."

He glanced over at her, his expression etched in light and shadows from the snow-covered night. "I don't know yet why the lovely Bennetts were trying to take Scotty. But I sure plan on finding out. Devon is working on that right now and someone from CHAIM should be taking care of our friendly neighbors even as I speak. Hopefully, they will give us some answers. In the meantime, I'm getting y'all as far away from Maine as I can."

"Which means?"

"Which means that's all you need to know right now."

"You suspected this before you came, right?"

"I told you that, yes."

"But you weren't very clear with details. I need details, Eli."

"I don't have the details," he replied, hitting his big hand on the steering wheel. "And that's the thing that's driving me crazy." Then he gave her a tight smile. "Not crazy like I was after…after South America, mind you. But just crazy enough to take matters into my own hands."

His cell phone rang then, causing both of them to start. "*Oui?*"

"I can't locate an agent right away. But I've put out an alert. We might have to let the Bennetts go for now."

"I don't like that."

"Just keep moving. And let me talk to Gena."

Frustrated, Eli shoved the phone at her. "Your brother wants to talk to you."

Gena took the phone. "Devon, what's going on?"

"I don't know yet," her brother said, his voice calming in her ear. "We're going to figure this out, okay? I just wanted to make sure you and Scotty are safe."

"We're okay for now. Just a bit shaken."

"I wish I could take care of this for you, but you can trust Eli. He loves Scotty."

"I know," she said, looking over at the man driving them away from their home. "It's just hard. It's Christmas and Scotty's so confused and afraid."

"I'm sure you both are, but listen to Eli."

"Okay. I guess I don't have any other choice."

"Not for now. Just hang tight. He's taking you to a safe place."

"He won't explain—"

"He can't explain right now. Try to understand."

"All right."

"Lydia and I love you both and you have our prayers."

"Same here," she said. "Bye." She handed the phone back to Eli and listened as he grunted and nodded his head.

She knew he wouldn't tell her what he and Devon had discussed, but she imagined her brother was reinforcing that he needed to keep them safe. She had no doubt Eli was capable of doing that, but she couldn't help her resentment. He had brought trouble to her door, hadn't he? Or had he truly come into their lives at just the right time?

Help me to understand and trust, Lord, she prayed. *Keep my son safe, please.*

Eli reached a hand over to her. "It's going to be all right. You have to believe that."

"I'm trying," she said, the warmth of his hand over hers and his gentle tone giving her a small measure of strength. "But Scotty's had a secure, steady routine up until—"

"Until I showed up," he said, nodding. "I'm sorry for that. I'm just glad I went with my gut and came to you."

The way he said "came to you" sent little flutters throughout Gena's system. As if he'd known instinctively they were destined to find each other just as she'd felt when he'd held her last night. *Stop it,* she told herself. He was referring to Scotty, of course. He'd come here for Scotty's sake and now he was stuck with her as part of the package.

And that was the part that worried Gena the most. What if Eli didn't want her as part of the package? What if he was just biding his time until he saw his way clear to take full custody of his son? What would become of her life then?

Eli patted her hand. "Let me get us on down the road and we'll find a place to spend the night. We have to be careful."

"You mean this isn't over yet?"

"No, I'm afraid not. I can tell you that much at least. Whoever is behind this is just getting started."

"That Bennett man wouldn't tell me anything either," she said, remembering the terror of finding him in Scotty's room. "And I'm pretty sure if he'd taken us with him, I'd be dead right now."

"You're too smart for your own good," Eli replied, a solid fear in his eyes. "But you're probably right."

"You don't have to sugarcoat things for me, Eli. I'm a big girl."

"And used to being independent," he said with a grin. "I'm glad you're on my side for sure, *chère*."

Gena leaned close. "Just remember that when you think about doing something without clueing me in, okay?"

"Yes, ma'am." Then he turned gentle on her. "Close your eyes, *belle*. Try to rest."

"I can't rest."

He laced his fingers through hers. "Close your eyes."

Gena did as he said, but she knew she wouldn't sleep.

Eli started humming. The tune was both poignant and soothing.

"What is it?" Gena asked, a melancholy falling over her.

"*J'ai passé par votre porte.* 'I Passed by Your Door,'" he told her. "It's a very old Cajun song."

"It's pretty, but it sounds almost sad."

"That's true," he replied. "Maybe because that's the way you look to me right now."

Gena opened her eyes to find him glancing at her, his hand still in hers. He turned back to the road, but he held her hand there in the dark and hummed to her until she finally did fall asleep.

Then she woke to the sound of tires grinding and screeching and the truck careening off the road.

SEVEN

"**B**lowout!" Eli shouted as he held the steering wheel and turned it back into the skid. "Bennett must have messed with my tires."

Gena held on, one hand automatically going behind her to push at Scotty's down jacket. "Hold tight, baby," she shouted to her frightened son.

Eli gripped the wheel and tapped the brakes until they skidded through bramble to a fast stop right into a snow drift, the impact jarring them against their seat belts, then back against the seats. Silence filled the truck before Eli released a breath. "That was close. Everyone okay in here?"

Gena nodded. "Scotty, are you all right?"

"Yes" came the quiet reply. "Are the bad guys still after us?"

Eli glanced over at Gena. "No. Just a slight problem with a flat tire. I'll have that fixed in no time."

Gena heard the unspoken words in Eli's tone. *He hoped.* The big truck was buried in about two feet of snow. How could he even get to the flat to fix it?

"Sit tight while I check things out," Eli said, reaching across the seat for Scotty's hockey stick. "To move snow," he explained.

Gena knew better than that. He might have to use that hockey stick as a weapon again if they were being followed. Praying that no one was behind them, she glanced around the woods. They'd landed in a flat meadow centered between several craggy hills and rocks. Gena figured Eli's expert handling of the wheel had saved them from crashing into those rocks.

She could see his silhouette in the gray moonlight, her heart pounding with adrenaline and fear. What if someone was lurking out there? Maybe she should get out and help him. She turned to Scotty. "Stay right here, honey, okay?"

Scotty bobbed his head. "Don't go far, Mom."

"I'm going to help Eli." She opened the door on her side and fell into the deep snow. "Eli?"

He called out to her. "Get back inside. This is gonna take a while."

Gena hopped back into the truck and scooted to the driver door then lowered the window. "I can at least help you. It's freezing out there."

"I'm aware of that," he shot back, his tone full of sarcasm. "No need for both of us to be cold. Just stay with Scotty and let me figure this out."

Gena heard the command in his words. Men didn't want to be bothered with questions and ideas when they were in their commander mode. And this one was especially independent and bull-headed. She sat silent, glancing back at her son.

He looked around the truck, then smiled at her. "Mr. Eli has a big first aid kit, Mom. Maybe there's something in there that would help."

"Good idea," Gena replied, reaching to where Scotty pointed on the back floor. Hefting the heavy metal kit, she opened it, then turned the truck key so she could have power from the interior light up on the rearview mirror. The kit had the usual things—bandage and antiseptic and such. But Gena noticed right away this was no ordinary kit. It was a survival kit, complete with plastic tarps and rain slickers, knives and other gadgets, matches and flint and even lip balm and lotion.

"Always prepared," she said in a low whisper. What kind of life was that for a man?

The kind your own husband and your brother both chose, she reminded herself. After Richard's death, she'd vowed to never get involved with anyone remotely close to being a secret agent of any kind. Yet here she sat, in a snowdrift in the middle of nowhere with Eli Trudeau. On the run with Eli Trudeau, at that.

Lifting things up, she noticed something else tucked in the box. A picture of her son. He must have taken it from one of her scrapbooks and hidden it here.

"Mom, did you find something?"

"No, honey. Not anything that can help right now."

Eli knocked on the window. Gena quickly closed the first aid box. "How bad is it?"

"Pretty bad," he said. "I looked around. So far, no one has come to visit. But I'm sure they're close by. That's the good news. The bad—they took my spare. So even if I could get to the flat to change it, which I can't, we don't have another tire." He heaved a breath. "And I can't get a signal on my cell."

Gena remembered he'd made her leave her cell behind because he didn't think the line was clear. She inhaled the frigid air. "We're stuck here?"

He leaned in, bringing the cold with him. "I didn't say

that, now, did I?" He glanced around. "The GPS system can tell us where the nearest town is, and if it works the way it's supposed to, I might be able to patch in an SOS to CHAIM. If they can get through, they'll see the truck's signal and leave directions for us from here. In the meantime, we can walk out of here if we have to. My cell is fully equipped for just about any kind of communication, if I can get through to the main network."

"We're going to walk in the middle of the night, in this weather?" Gena shook her head. She had a feeling this was just the tip of the iceberg.

"That's better than being sitting ducks for these people, Gena. Dev told me to stay on the move and I'd feel better if we did. I have to protect both of you."

"What are you guys talking about, Mom?"

Gena turned to her son. "We might have to walk somewhere to find help. Think you're up to it?"

"Sure," Scotty said. But he didn't sound so sure.

Eli tapped a hand on the seat. "Your mom told me you're a Cub Scout. This will be a true test of your mettle. Like a big adventure."

Scotty lifted his head. "Can I take my hockey stick?"

"And your skates," Eli said. "Might need them to get over some thin ice."

Gena knew he wasn't referring to frozen water. They had no real weapons to speak of. They had to be creative.

"I missed Santa," Scotty said, unhooking his seat belt. "And now I can't even open my other presents."

Gena saw the regret in Eli's eyes. "When we get to where we're going, I'll make sure Santa finds you there."

"Okay."

Gena hurt for the acceptance in Scotty's lone word. Her

son had always accepted things easily. He never complained, never asked too many questions. But she knew he had questions, lots of them. And she had no idea how to explain all of this to him.

Eli motioned for her to move over. "Let me check the GPS and see what's what."

After punching buttons and studying the computerized system on the dash, he said, "It looks like we're about ten miles from the interstate. And I don't see much in the way of help between here and there and I'm not picking up an immediate response from my signal through to the CHAIM satellite. If we can make it to the main road, we might find a lodge or hotel at least."

"Ten miles. That's a long way in freezing temperatures."

"Good thing we dressed warm then." He touched a finger to her cheek. "We have to do this, Gena. I feel too exposed sitting out here in the moonlight. At least the snow's let up."

Gena couldn't celebrate even that small victory. The moonlit night looked eerie and treacherous to her—like a frozen prison. She didn't want to think about the long trek ahead of them.

But Eli was already gathering supplies, including the first aid kit. "Just in case," he said as he got out again and came around the truck to get Scotty. "Okay, make sure you have on your hat and mittens and that muffler around your face. We don't want your *maman* worrying about you, now do we?"

Scotty was already bundled and ready to go, his eyes the only thing showing underneath his thick hat and wool muffler.

Eli pointed to some low bushes near the rocks a few yards away. "Go right over there and hide behind those shrubs, but stay where I can see you. Hold on while I construct a little detour for anyone who might try to mess with my truck." He hurried around to the back and got something out of the tool box. Gena couldn't tell what he was rigging and she didn't want to know. She just wanted to get out of here.

"C'mon, Scotty," she said, guiding her bundled son over to the edge of the woods.

She watched as Eli moved around the truck for several minutes, winding something that looked like a thin wire throughout the bramble and rocks near where they'd landed. Then he hurried over to them. "I might have to go back out there, so we need to find a more secure spot to hide you two."

"Why's the truck still running?" Scotty asked, looking up at Eli.

Eli glanced toward Gena, then gave his son an explanation. "I want anyone who shows up to think we're still in the truck, so I left it cranked. If we're being followed, this should flush them out."

Gena could only imagine what sort of innovative technique Eli had used to make the truck a decoy. As long as it protected Scotty, she could live with it.

"You hold on to me or your mama at all times, understand?" Eli said to Scotty as he took the boy's hand. "We're going to walk the perimeters of the field, sticking close to the woods."

Scotty nodded. "Yes, sir."

"And if I say run or duck down or hide, you do as I say, all right?"

Again, the boy nodded.

"I think we're gonna make it just fine, but we just need some rules here." Eli glanced at Gena. "Imagine that, me reciting rules. I've never had much use for them before."

Gena didn't want to tell him what she thought of his rules. Her son was in danger. That's all she could think about. But she wrapped her wool scarf around her neck and pulled the matching cap down over her ears. "I just want us safe and warm."

"Then let's get cracking." Eli pulled things out of the various pockets of his heavy coat, then crammed as many supplies as he could pack into his large backpack. "The snow is deep in places. Take care."

Scotty took Gena's hand, then turned to Eli and reached out the other one to him. "I'm ready."

Eli lifted Scotty's hockey stick over one shoulder and slung his tied skates over the other, then took Scotty's hand.

"Want me to carry something?" Scotty asked, looking up at Eli.

Eli sent a gentle glance toward Gena, then shook his head. "*Non,* I just need you to hold on to me, okay?"

Scotty stayed silent, his bright eyes trusting as he stared up at Eli.

Gena thought her heart would burst with fear and regret. She didn't know whether Eli had come here as a saint or a hindrance, but she was glad he was with them right now. Because if these people, whoever they were, had taken her son from her, she would have gone mad with grief and worry. *Just as Eli had,* she thought as she watched his face now. She immediately understood what he must have felt, thinking his wife and unborn child were both dead. Then she thought about the picture of Scotty inside the first aid kit.

Without realizing her actions, Gena squeezed his hand tight as they started up the slight incline toward the narrow country road. Eli gave her a quick look, then held her gloved fingers tight against the leather of his own gloves.

"Je vous maintiendrai sûr," he whispered into her ear. "I will take care of you."

Gena wanted to believe that gentle promise with all her heart, but the night wind and the high white moon only reinforced their exposure and their isolation.

And then Gena heard a car screeching to a halt up the road, followed by the flash of something glinting in the moonlight, coming through the other side of the woods about a hundred yards away. A tiny beam of light, maybe?

Eli had seen it, too. He tugged at her hand, then bent down to Scotty. "Can you run fast?"

Scotty bobbed his head, looking up at Gena.

"Hold on," Eli said. "We're going to make a run for that spot of trees over there across the road."

Scotty and Gena both started out. Gena could hear the truck's frustrated whines in the background. The big vehicle was roaring and loud—a souped-up version of a normal truck. Hopefully, the sound and facade of someone being behind the wheel would distract whoever was out there.

"Run now," Eli said as he pulled them along.

Gena's heart rate accelerated with all the intensity of an avalanche, but she did as Eli told her. And she held on to her son and his father for dear life.

Eli pushed them down into the low, snow-covered shrubs. "Stay down," he said, his gaze scanning the open white field in front of them. "Hopefully, they didn't see us in time to figure out we're not sitting in the truck. We were so close to the tree line, I'm thinking our footsteps blended right in."

"Did it work?" Scotty asked.

"I think it did at that," Eli replied, trying to keep his tone light in spite of the drumbeat of pulse echoing inside his ears. "Let's just catch our breath and try to figure out our next move. If we go around this field and then cut back, we can find the road again."

He looked over at Gena and saw that she was shivering. "C'mere," he said tugging her close as he settled them underneath the protection of a cluster of chokeberry bushes centered between two tall birch trees.

Gena pushed Scotty toward Eli. "Sit between us, baby, so we can keep you warm."

"It's pretty dry under here," Eli said, pulling Scotty up against one of the birch tree's white trunk. He put an arm around Scotty, then urged Gena close. "Sit tight."

Gena leaned in toward her son. Eli put his arm around her shoulder as they formed a cocoon of waterproof coats and wool scarves and mufflers around the boy. "I have to say, I've never done this before," he whispered, hoping to distract both of them. "I mean, I've been stuck in cold and snow, but never with such a pretty mom and her brave son." And he had hoped he'd never have to put them through this.

"Where did they go?" Scotty asked in a whisper.

"Not sure," Eli replied. "Let's stay still and quiet and maybe we'll hear something."

He leaned forward, squinting through the bramble, then turned to dig inside his backpack until he found his binoculars.

"Can you see?" Scotty asked, craning his neck.

"I can, indeed. Night-vision binoculars. Very high-powered." The batteries were new and could last twenty hours at least. And these sweet babies could bring in anything moving within a thousand feet.

"What do you see, Mr. Eli?"

"Shh." Gena put a finger to her lips. "Try to be still and quiet, honey."

Scotty did as she told him, but he kept his eyes on Eli.

Eli scanned the field and the woods, spotting almost immediately the interlopers on the other side. Whoever was out there was trekking toward his truck, just as he'd figured they would. That didn't bode well. He knew what they'd try to do if they found out no one was inside—probably destroy his truck to hide any trace of their being here. Which was why he'd beaten them to the draw. He'd at least set them back a bit by taking matters into his own hands. But that was a mighty fine new truck he'd bought purposely for this trip. At least he'd put everything he could carry in his big sturdy backpack. Force of habit.

He watched, the cold settling around him like a wet towel, as two darkly dressed figures came out of the woods and shuffled through the snow. Even though they'd shut off their lights, as they crouched near edge of the field, Eli had a clear view of them. Looked to both be male. And they were carrying weapons. One had a rifle and the other one had a bow and arrow. These people meant business.

Eli kept his eyes trained on the two men. He knew they wouldn't kill Scotty because they wanted the boy. But they certainly would kill him. Nothing new, that. He'd made enough people mad to have a list of predators lined up after him. And he also knew that they'd kill Gena or take her with them and then kill her. He couldn't let that happen, of course. He wouldn't let any of it happen.

But he wasn't sure how he was going to save them. The wind chill had to be close to zero and the moonlight was like a beacon shining down on the white field and bare trees on both sides of the narrow road. They could stay warm for a little while, but soon things would get nasty.

"Eli?"

He heard the worry in Gena's voice.

"I'm thinking, *chère*. Just trying to form a plan once I take care of these two."

He watched as the pair moved along the tree line, trying to stay out of sight. They made it to the back of the roaring truck, each hunched low on either side.

Just as one of the men duckwalked his way to the passenger door, his weapon at the ready, Eli decided it was now or never.

"Listen up," he said to Gena and Scotty. "In about a minute I'm going to run back toward the truck and I'm going to light a bottle and throw it at those men. It's going to explode and make a lot of noise. I wrapped a tiny wire across the bushes surrounding each door. When they turn to run from the flames and noise, I'm going to tug on that wire and they should get all tripped up. And when they do, I want you both to make a run south toward the other end of this field. Understand?"

They both bobbed their heads.

Eli gathered his supplies and then slowly lifted up, bringing Scotty with him. "We run and we don't look back, okay?"

"Okay," Scotty said.

"Eli, I'm not sure—"

Gena didn't get to finish her sentence. Eli pushed Scotty at her, then took off. Quickly lighting the gasoline-soaked rag he'd stuffed around a capped glass bottle, he threw the bomb into the air, aiming it right for the side of the truck where the men crouched. There was a loud boom and then the ground around the truck went up in flames. Eli heard a grunt and watched as the two men rushed back toward the cover of the rocks and bushes and straight into the thin cables he'd rigged across the bramble. Grabbing the end of the wire where he'd left it in the bushes, Eli tugged hard to bring it up to knee level. They both went down right onto the rocks and ice, hitting hard from the groans he heard echoing through the night.

He waited only to make sure neither of them got back up. This trick had worked before, so he hoped he hadn't lost his touch. The flames would die out soon, though. And the men would get up and start hunting them again.

"Let's go," he said, grabbing Scotty up in his arms. Then he tossed Gena Scotty's tied skates. "Run, Gena. Keep running until we reach those woods! We'll catch up."

He pushed her ahead of him and held on to Scotty as they hurried across the snow, watching behind him and looking ahead to make sure she was almost there.

Halfway across the field, he heard Gena's intake of breath as she came to a halt a few feet ahead of him. "Eli, this isn't snow anymore. We're on a frozen lake."

And right after she said it, Eli heard the jagged, laughing sound of ice cracking.

EIGHT

Gena turned, then stopped, holding out a hand toward Eli. "Don't come any farther. Let me come back to you."

Eli gasped and held tight to Scotty. "Gena—"

"Stay there," she said in a low hiss. "I know what to do."

She could tell he was wrestling with that. He needed to be the rescuer, but this time he was going to have to listen to her. Or they could all wind up in the cold water.

Taking a deep breath, she listened as the ice crack grew louder. In a few seconds, she was going under whether she liked it, unless she could get herself out of this. Looking toward the shore, she took a step, careful not to retrace her previous steps. Telling herself they were still close enough to the shore for the water to be shallow, Gena prayed that if she fell through, at least she'd only get her feet wet at the most. She'd taken two more steps when the spot where she'd been standing caved.

"Run," Eli said in a low whisper. "Gena, please—"

"Mommy!"

She didn't run. Gena closed her mind to the fear in her son's call as she flattened herself down on the ice. She slowly laid Scotty's skates aside, then started to belly crawl back to Eli and Scotty. Behind her, the ice gave way inch by inch, cracks forming like a snake hissing and whipping toward her. She kept her mind on getting back to the shore.

After what seemed an eternity, she looked up to find Eli's hand extended toward her, with Scotty standing right beside him. "Take it!" he said, his voice raw with frustration and concern.

Gena reached toward his outstretched hand as he lurched back to pull her up, causing all three of them to fall on the snow-covered ground. They all looked up just in time to see the ice open wide in the spot where she'd been standing just minutes before. And Scotty's new skates disappeared inside the cavernous hole.

Eli held to her on one side and his son on the other, his backpack bracing them. "Are you all right?"

Gena nodded, her heart still pounding. A shiver started at the top of her head and worked its way down her spine. "I'm fine," she said between chattering teeth. "Just so cold."

Eli kissed the top of her wool cap. "Can you walk?"

"Yes." Then she lifted up. "Scotty, I'm okay, honey. We have to keep moving."

"Just not out there," Scotty replied on a pragmatic note.

"No, not out there," Eli said, lifting up with a grunt as he held on to Scotty, then turned to give Gena his hand again. "I thought I was going to have a heart attack."

In spite of her close call, Gena smiled. "And here I thought you could be calm in any situation."

"I hate ice," he said by way of an explanation. "And I just didn't know what to do for you."

"You would have figured it out," she said, knowing that he would have saved her no matter the cost to himself. Then she realized why he'd been so rattled. In order to save her, he would have had to leave Scotty alone and vulnerable on the shore. That had been his dilemma. Touched that he'd given her a chance to help herself before abandoning her son, Gena knew she could count on Eli to do the right thing if push came to shove. Just to reassure herself and him, she said, "I'm fine. Now let's get going."

Eli nodded, then moved Scotty to Gena's side. "I need to check and make sure our friends aren't following us."

Scotty rushed to Gena, hugging her legs. "I was scared for you, Mom."

"I was scared for me, too," Gena said, bending to hold him close. "But I knew I had both of you to help me."

"My skates are gone," Scotty said into her coat collar. "I didn't even get to try them out."

"I know, honey. I'll get you another pair and another hockey stick, too, I promise."

She felt his head moving against her shoulder, her heart beat picking back up as she thought about what would become of him if something happened to her. He had Eli now and that gave her some reassurance. And he had Devon and Lydia, too. But she couldn't stop shaking.

Then she felt Eli's hand on her other shoulder. "All clear. The fire's out and so are our visitors. We need to get moving."

She nodded, taking Scotty's hand in hers. "I don't hear the truck running anymore."

"Probably out of gas. The diversion I set up should give us time to get farther away. Those two might not be too hurt, but they'll be slowed down some."

Gena noticed both the gun and the bow he now carried, but she didn't question him on either.

He took Scotty back in his arms, then laced his fingers in hers. "Ready?"

Gena inhaled, her lungs hurting with the effort. "Yes."

They walked around the woods, careful to stay close to the bramble and trees. The moon was up high now. The pull of fatigue moved throughout Gena's body. Her feet were so numb she couldn't feel her shoes and her nose hurt from the freezing air. She looked over at Eli and saw that Scotty had fallen asleep in his arms.

"Is he…?"

"He's warm," Eli said. "He's keeping me warm."

Gena shivered in relief, but Eli misinterpreted the shiver. He pulled her close. "Hold your face against my jacket."

Gena did as he said, snuggling against him and keeping her eyes toward the ground as they slowly made their way around the woods and lake. Then she felt him nudge her. "Look, up ahead."

Gena lifted her head and stepped away from Eli. "It's an ice fishing hut!"

Eli let out a relieved breath. "Shelter."

"Shelter," she said, smiling up at him. "It's close to the shore, so we should be safe from falling through. And if we're really blessed, we'll have warmth from a propane lamp or stove, too."

"Warmth," he said, touching a gloved finger to her nose. "That would be very nice right about now."

Together, they made their way toward the square, squatty little hut and Gena prayed they wouldn't find any more surprises waiting for them there.

The little plywood and metal hut was sparse in its decorating scheme but sturdy and dry. After he'd made sure they were on solid ice, Eli pushed Gena inside, then spotted a bench bed with a foam mattress on one side of the small structure. Taking Scotty there, he carefully laid the boy down and tugged off his wet boots. Gena found an old wool blanket on a shelf and placed that over Scotty.

"He's worn out," Eli said, his own bones groaning from this night's efforts.

Gena nodded, busy with bringing two fold-up chairs close together. "We have a lantern and a kerosene heater, at least. And I think I see some soup cans up on the shelf."

Eli turned to where she pointed. "We can warm it over the heater. And our feet, too."

Together, they set about gathering supplies and heating a can of chicken noodle soup. Soon, Gena had a folding table out to go with the chairs.

Eli sat down, a cup of steaming soup in his hand, then handed her the other one. "Drink up."

Gena looked over at Scotty. "I guess I should let him sleep. We have the crackers and power bars I packed for later."

"He needs to rest right now," Eli said, nodding. Then he looked over at her. She seemed drained, her dark eyes bright with worry for her son. "I'm sorry I've put you both through this."

She stared over at him, her fingers gripping her mug. "Do you have any idea what's going on, Eli?"

"I have a few theories, *oui.*"

"Want to share them with me?"

He took a sip of his soup. "For now, all you need to know is this—someone is after Scotty for some reason."

"And you think you might be that reason?"

He let out a grunt. "I'm usually the reason for something bad going on."

He hated the sympathy and the doubt he saw in her eyes. But her next words encouraged him.

"Eli, I'm on your side. You have to talk to me."

He'd never heard that one before. The only other people in the world who'd ever believed in him were now dead. His mother and his wife had both loved him in spite of his anger and torment. And Lydia, of course. Very much alive and well, Lydia Cantrell had brought Eli to a new place in his faith journey. She'd tell him to level with Gena and let God take care of the rest.

He glanced over at his son, then looked at the woman beside him. "I never knew my father," he explained, his voice quiet and centered as he stared at the gas lantern's flickering flames. "He never got a chance to marry my mother."

"What do you mean?"

"He never knew she was pregnant with me."

Gena didn't flinch or look disgusted by that, so he continued. "My papa, Edward Savoy, came from a very wealthy Louisiana family. He met my *maman* at a children's home when he went to do some community service work for his college fraternity. It was her last year there as she was about to turn eighteen. They fell in love and planned to marry. But when his father, Pierre, found out, he stopped all of that. He made my daddy enlist in CHAIM and sent him away for good, determined to teach him a lesson. My father was killed just a few months after he went into active service for CHAIM. My mother never heard from him again, so she raised me the best she could. She took me to a little island in south Louisiana and she found work as a waitress. Sometimes, she worked two jobs, but we got by. I grew up in the swamps and on that island."

He inhaled a deep breath, then put his empty cup on the table. "When I had just started community college, a man approached me and told me he was my grandfather, Pierre Savoy. He talked about my papa and how much I was like him. He also talked to me about serving in this secret organization—the same organization my father had served in—CHAIM." He looked up, staring at Scotty. "I wanted to be like my father, wanted to be brave and good. I figured my mother would be proud and so would my grandfather. My mother passed on before I could do her proud. And as for my grandfather—I was so wrong about him."

Gena let out a gasp. "And, of course, you joined up to prove something to him."

"*Oui*, but once I was inside, the man only tormented me even more. That man was the Peacemaker, a very high official in CHAIM. He died in Colorado earlier this year, but before he died, he tried to kill Devon, Lydia and me."

"And you took a bullet to save them. That's all Devon would ever tell me."

He nodded. "I was ready to die. To get it over with. But…Devon gave me a reason to live."

He pointed to Scotty. "From the time I was able, after I got shot, I planned on coming to find my son. And in the meantime, I got these funny feelings. Then Kissie mentioned some chatter coming through the CHAIM network. Apparently, that mess down in Rio Branco had a domino effect that's still causing trouble. People were asking around about me. The Peacemaker was the head honcho down there, so it stood to reason he'd have a backup plan if anything happened to him. Call it bad vibes or instinct or as Lydia would say, a sign from God, but I knew I had to get here and find my boy. I had to help him."

"I understand that," Gena said, taking his hand. "And I want Scotty to know you, but I can't help but think if you'd stayed away—"

He grabbed her by the shoulders. "You don't get it, do

you? That old man was evil—I mean truly evil. I think he's still pulling the strings from his grave. I think he knew where Scotty was all along and he'd just been biding his time. He tracked me down. What was to stop him from doing the same thing with my son? If he hadn't died in Colorado—if I had died—then you probably wouldn't have Scotty today."

She pushed at his hands. "What are you saying?"

"I'm trying to tell you that I think he left instructions for someone to come and find my son, to get back at me, or worse he left someone mad enough to get even somehow. And I don't even want to think what that could mean for Scotty."

"Why would you think that? He's dead. What could he or anyone else possibly gain from something like that?"

Eli pulled her close, his gaze moving over her face. How could he explain this? Finally, he told her the one thing he knew for sure. "The old man left his entire estate to me, Gena. And that just doesn't make any sense. He hated me, so why would he leave everything he owned to me?"

She shook her head. "Maybe he wanted to make amends."

"No." Eli held her there, hoping to make her see. "In spite of his code name, the Peacemaker wasn't the type of man to make amends. He always had a plan, an agenda. And I believe he still has one. And it involves getting even with me. And what do you think the best way for him to do that would be, *chère?*"

Gena moaned, going limp in his arms. "To take your child," she whispered, her skin pale against the lamp's flame. "Bennett said something like that to me in Scotty's room. He said something like…this was supposed to be easy, but *you* got in the way. Oh, Eli, what would I have done if you hadn't come in time?"

"I'm here now," he said, pulling her into his arms. He stroked her vanilla-scented hair, then lifted her chin. "I'm here now and I'm taking you and Scotty back to Louisiana with me. I'm going to find out what else that old man left to me—or for me."

"How can that help?"

Eli's body shuddered with regret and pain. "Because I'm pretty sure that whatever he left behind was purposely put there to incriminate me, to have me put away for good. He's still out to destroy me, one way or another."

He held Gena close, his mind whirling with all the possibilities. He'd either inherited an evil legacy or he'd inherited something he could use to make things right. If he could just figure out what it all meant.

And if he could just protect Gena and their son from ever having to witness that evil.

NINE

Gena awoke to morning sunlight streaming through the tiny smudged windows of the hut. Blinking, she moved her hand up the solid arm nestled next to her.

Eli!

Pushing up, she realized they'd held each other all night long, sitting straight up in their jackets and wool caps against the bench bed with Scotty asleep right beside them. No wonder she felt so safe and warm. Eli had covered Scotty with an extra blanket and opened his own big down coat to include Gena, his arms wrapped around her while she slept.

"Hello," he said, his eyes moving over her face with an unreadable intensity. Then he touched a hand to her temple. "You have a sleep mark right there."

"I don't doubt that," she said, running her fingers over the crease. "I can't believe I slept at all."

He got up and eased away, then stretched. "It was a long night."

"Meaning you didn't sleep," she said, knowing he'd probably sat there watching over them all night long.

"I'm used to little sleep, *belle*. Don't worry about me."

Gena wanted to tell him that she did worry about him.

She never thought she'd even feel that way, but Eli had a way of getting to her. He was all male, fierce and protective and dangerous, but he also had his own code of honor and that code meant he'd die for those he loved. He'd come close to it already, hadn't he? And that quality endeared her to him in a way that only made her think of Richard and how much she'd loved him.

Her heart couldn't go through that kind of pain ever again.

"What are you thinking with such a frown on that pretty face?" he asked as he went through his backpack, then handed her a granola bar.

"I don't know," she admitted. But she didn't dare tell him what she was really thinking. "Where do we go from here?"

He stared out the high window. "Well, we didn't have any visitors during the night, so I'd say whoever is out there didn't spot this hut or they're going to plan B. Which means we have to do the same."

"What is plan B?" she said as she stared down at her untouched food.

"First, we get off this block of ice. Then we head toward the highway. I'm gonna try and find us some transportation. If I can get a line to Devon and if he got my distress signal earlier, we might make a connection with some local CHAIM members."

"Local?" Gena got up. "You mean you have members here in Maine?"

"*Oui*. Devon knew that when he brought the boy to you. I mean, your own husband was a native, right? Stands to reason he would have had people in place to watch out for you. And after he died—"

"Devon knew that and knew Scotty would be relatively

safe here, even if he didn't bother telling me the entire plan." Then she spun around to glare at him. "Which also means you didn't have to come all this way to check on us."

"Yes, I did." He pointed to Scotty. "Because of him."

"You didn't trust your own organization?"

"That's about the way of it, yes." He leaned close. "Does that concern you?"

Gena pushed at her hair. "Why should all this espionage and all these secrets concern me, Eli? I mean, it's just my life you've all been playing with, right? It's just your son's life."

Eli sent a warning glance toward Scotty.

Turning, Gena sighed with relief that she hadn't woken her son with those harsh, telling words. "I can't deal with this. Let's just get out of here, okay?"

He stopped her, pulling her around to face him. "I'm sorry, but you should be glad we were watching out for you. You don't have to do this all on your own, Gena. Devon knew that and even I—stubborn man that I am— certainly understand it. Why is it so hard for you to accept that we all care about you and the boy?"

Gena thought about that, her heart blazing with all that CHAIM had done in the name of watching out for her. "Well, let me think about that. I lost my husband to CHAIM and then I gained a son because of CHAIM. And now, I've gained your presence here and even more danger at my door. And I'm supposed to be thankful for that."

He looked angry. "I thought you'd at least be thankful for Scotty."

Gena let out a gasp of air. "You know how I feel about him, so don't even bring that up. It's just that—" She sank down on a chair. "It's just that until all of this came back into my life—all this CHAIM business—Scotty and I were doing pretty good. We were safe and happy."

She saw the hurt in Eli's dark eyes. Her words and tone indicated what she'd said to him from the very beginning. She blamed him for this, no matter what he'd try to tell her. Gena knew that was true and she knew it wasn't fair to him, but she had to have something to cling to, to keep her sanity if nothing else.

He turned cold, his eyes going so dark she knew she'd hurt him to the very core. "You were never that safe," he said, "and as for happiness, well, trust me, that's just an illusion. So get over it for now."

Eli stomped through the woods, careful to stay alert and aware of his surroundings. If his compass and the sun were any indicators, they should hit a southbound highway any minute now. He held Scotty's hand in his, afraid to let go of the boy for even a second, while Gena trailed behind, silent and watchful.

She hated him. He knew that from the way she'd talked earlier inside that cramped little hut. It didn't take much to figure she blamed him for this trek through the frozen tundra. And why shouldn't she just fall in line behind everyone else who'd blamed him for all the wrongs in their life? His grandfather certainly had and Eli was still paying for that. And even Devon had tried to pin the blame on Eli when someone was trying to kill him last year, until Eli had shown him that he wasn't behind that. His grandfather, Pierre Savoy, was the one trying to kill both of them. Now, Gena.

Gena. He'd hoped, thought that she was going to be different. But then, that was before he'd had to take her and Scotty out of their controlled, sheltered environment and bring them out into the cold harsh reality of what being on the run truly meant. Would he ever find any peace?

"How much farther?" Scotty asked, his breath fogging up as he spoke.

"About a mile," Eli said, grinning down at him. "You are for sure a good hiker."

"Mom and I like to take long walks."

Eli glanced back to Gena. "Is that right?"

She didn't respond. She just kept on walking.

"How are you doing back there?" Eli asked to make conversation.

"I'm fine."

But she wasn't fine. He could hear that in her tone, see it in her body language. After last night, he'd thought maybe... Well, forget last night. They'd been cold and tired and they'd clung to what comfort they could find. No matter that she'd sat curled against him as if she trusted him with all her heart. No matter that his son had been sleeping there, safe and nearby, and that for a brief instance, Eli could picture this type of thing in his mind for a long time. Them, all three of them, together, curled up by a fire, warm and safe and happy. Not out in some isolated, freezing hut on the run, but home together, watching a funny movie, eating popcorn, then falling asleep, safe and happy and trusting.

What a stupid, silly daydream.

He was still lost inside that dream when he heard a twig snap somewhere in the forest behind them.

Eli stopped, swung around. "Did you hear that?" he asked Gena, wondering if he'd lost his touch after all. No, but he was mightily distracted by this woman and what she was making him face.

"I think I heard something," she whispered back, her eyes meeting his for the first time since they'd left the hut.

"Follow me," he said, the unnecessary command force of habit. He guided them over to a copse of dense bramble and thick saplings by a cluster of pine trees. "Get down."

Scotty did as he was told. Gena automatically took her son into her arms as she sank down beside Eli. "What is it?"

Eli shook his head. "Can't be sure. Let's just sit tight for a minute."

He got out his binoculars to scan the distant woods. "We're so close to finding civilization, maybe if someone's out there they'll just keep wandering."

Then he saw something, just a brief movement.

"A deer," he said, dropping the binoculars as the big doe came within view. "See her, Scotty. She's looking for breakfast."

Scotty let out a "Wow. Look, Mom."

"I see," Gena said, excitement in her voice. She glanced over at Eli. "We rarely see them around our house."

"She's facing the wind, so any predators won't pick up her scent," Eli said, remembering his hunting days back down in Louisiana. "And just like us right now, she won't ever sleep in the same place twice."

"You're comparing us to a wild deer?" Gena asked, a frown on her pretty face. But he saw the mirth in her eyes. And it was like a balm to his bruised soul.

"We're in survival mode, *oui*," he retorted. "And you can learn a lot from the wild creatures."

"I wish I had a fur coat," Scotty said, grinning.

Eli laughed at that, able to relax for just a brief minute. "She is a beautiful sight."

He looked over at Gena as he said that and was rewarded with a tilt of her head. Since her skin was red from the cold he couldn't tell if he'd made her blush. But he decided he was much better at flirting with her than trying to reason with her. Maybe that would be his best tactic for now.

"Guess we'd better leave her to her meal and get moving again," he said. "We should be very near a road. In fact, that's probably why our doe is here. She'd like the salt they use to deice the road."

"You sure know a lot about animals," Scotty said, clearly impressed.

"I grew up mostly outdoors," Eli replied, wishing he could tell his son all about his childhood. But he'd have to save that for a later time.

As they stood, the big doe lifted her head toward them, her nostrils flaring as she sensed danger.

"She's spotted us," Eli said, turning to pull Scotty along. Then because he felt the hair on the back of his neck standing up, he whirled back toward the deer.

She looked straight into his eyes and then away behind him before she lifted up and out into the air.

And that's when Eli felt the whiz of a bullet brushing past the pine tree branches just above his head.

He pushed at Scotty. "Get down!"

Gena fell to the ground, her body covering her son's on one side as Eli shielded them both as best he could.

"*That* wasn't a deer," Gena said, fear in her voice now.

"No. Someone's found us."

He rolled to his back, then grabbed at his binoculars again. After scanning the woods, he saw a lone hunter with a high-powered rifle moving slowly through the snow-covered bramble. "We have a visitor. And he probably brought a friend or two."

Scotty tried to raise his head, but Eli held him down. "Stay close to the ground, Scotty."

Scotty lay back down. Gena placed an arm around him. "It's okay, honey. We're in a good hiding spot."

"Are they gonna find us?"

"Not if I can help it," Eli said close to Scotty's ear. "I just have to figure out something."

He listened, honing in on his tracking instincts and his hunting knowledge. The deer had been smart, alerting them to the danger just beyond their hiding place and causing just enough of a distraction that the shot had missed. Maybe he should try to follow the deer. Or maybe she'd headed back deep into the woods.

Watching the man moving about a hundred yards away, Eli knew they had precious little time before their predator took aim again. His only chance was to distract the culprit until they could get to the highway. And he thought he knew a good way to do that.

Turning to Gena, he said, "Keep Scotty low to the ground. Don't move, no matter what happens, until I say so, okay?"

"What are you going to do?" Gena asked, nodding.

Eli started gathering nearby dry pine cones. "Cause a disturbance so we can get away."

Quickly, he placed the pine cones into the two wrinkled paper bags Gena had stuffed with snacks inside his backpack, then took his knife. "Stay here," he said. "I'll be back in a minute."

Giving them one last look, Eli crawled through the bramble, careful to be as quiet as possible, until he had the hunter in his sights. Then making sure he was in a hidden area, he gouged deep into a pine tree trunk and scraped out as much pine pitch as he could, then smeared it over the cones in the bag.

He slid silently across the cold earth, hurrying to get the bag hidden on the path near where the shot had passed. He'd have to cause a disturbance so the predator would turn toward the spot where he'd partially buried the bag of cones and resin. Satisfied that he'd done all he could, Eli crawled back to Gena and Scotty, then pulled out the bow and arrows he'd taken from one of the unconscious men last night after going back to his truck. "Now we wait."

"What did you do?" Gena asked.

"Too hard to explain," Eli replied, catching his breath. "Just remember, when I say go, we go."

He watched through the binoculars until the man was about fifty yards away from the bag of hidden pine cones. Then he rolled and grabbed a cone from nearby, wrapped it in another bag and crammed the whole thing on an arrow tip. Taking the lighter from the first aid kit, he touched it to the bag on the arrow.

"Get ready," he told Gena. Eli could see the man crouching low as he hurried through the woods toward where he'd heard the pine cone drop. Then Eli stood and took aim, firing the burning arrow right into the buried bags of sap-soaked cones.

In a matter of minutes, the resin-covered cones in one of the bags he'd hidden on the path lit up in a popping fire. And after that, the rest of the bags and cones caught on fire and made several loud popping sounds, followed by the return fire of the surprised hunter. That gave Eli time to reload his bow. This time he aimed for the hunter, hitting him in his lower left leg. The man went down, screaming in pain.

"Now," Eli said, pushing Gena and Scotty ahead of him. "Stay straight and don't look back." They wouldn't have a lot of time. But it was a chance, their only chance. Eli didn't want to use the gun unless he was forced to do so.

With one last prayer, he pushed them toward what he hoped would be a main highway, the sound of popping pine cones followed by gunshots echoing through the forest behind them.

TEN

Gena could hear screams of agony somewhere behind them, but following Eli's advice, she didn't dare look back as they stayed deep inside the trees and shrubs. Just when she thought she couldn't run any farther, they stumbled up a snow-covered embankment and onto a gray, salt-and-snow-encrusted highway.

"We made it," Eli said, Scotty in his arms. Looking over his shoulder, he scanned the woods behind them. "I think we lost him, but we have to keep moving."

He was out of breath from carrying the overstuffed backpack and his son. He'd kept her in front of him and he'd kept his solid back between Scotty and a bullet, holding Scotty's head against his chest as he ran.

"Let's get across the road and head toward that intersection up there." He pointed to a crossroads. "He won't be able to catch us with that wounded leg."

"That's all well and fine," she said, winded and tired as she rushed along. "But how do we get out of here?"

Eli stood Scotty up, then took the boy's hand, urging him to hurry. "Hopefully, I'll be able to contact Devon now—if our phones haven't been jammed."

They made it to the crossroads and Gena was relieved

to see a farmhouse and a barn in a clearing on the other side. "Maybe someone there can help us," she said, pointing toward the house.

Eli nodded, then sat Scotty on a tumbled-down tree's ancient broken trunk behind a thicket of saplings and bushes. "This is a pretty good hiding spot. I'm going to try Devon."

Gena waited, wondering what her brother was doing behind the scenes. Knowing Devon, he'd put out a state-wide CHAIM alert. She supposed her brother would never be completely free of this secretive organization and neither would she.

"You okay?" she asked her son.

Scotty bobbed his head. "Just tired. I wish we could go home."

"Soon," she said, silently promising to make that happen. "We just have to protect you from those bad guys."

"Why are they bothering us, Mom?"

"I don't know, honey. But…you've been so brave. So very brave. I need you to keep it up."

Sniffing from the cold, Scotty looked up at Eli. "I want to be just like him."

Gena's heart lurched at that comment. She wasn't so sure she wanted her son to be just like Eli Trudeau, but then Scotty did have the man's blood running through his veins. Watching Eli now, she marveled at how he always managed to figure a way out of any bad situation. He'd brought them this far at least. It made her think of that old saying about God not bringing you this far to let you down now. Thinking she was blessed to have both God and Eli on her side, Gena thanked the Lord for His love and asked Him to continue watching over them.

She held her son close and said a little prayer for his

safety, the same prayer that had been a constant in her mind since this had started.

Eli closed his phone and turned to them. "Good news. Devon is sending a CHAIM agent to find us and get us out of here and they found my truck, but...all of the culprits have suddenly disappeared. We need to go to that farmhouse and wait until dark when someone will contact us."

"Will they let us in?" Gena asked. "The people who live there?"

"They're not at home," he replied. "Already been cleared. I gave Dev our location and he did all the rest. He got verification that the house is empty—the owners are in Hilton Head for the winter."

"I don't even want to know how he did that," Gena replied, getting up to follow Eli up the ridge to the deserted farmhouse. She imagined satellites lurking in the sky, trained on them as they ran through the woods. She imagined listening devices and cameras and computers whirling with data. But she couldn't imagine herself caught up in this kind of life ever again. "I don't need to know," she said, almost to herself.

"Now you're learning," Eli retorted. "A need-to-know basis is the only way to travel with a CHAIM agent, *catin*."

Gena wanted to tell him that she *did* need to know a lot more than how they were getting into that farmhouse, but she refrained. She wouldn't question the man in front of her son.

Scotty apparently needed to know a few things of his own, however. "Mr. Eli, that was so cool. How'd you make those pine cones explode?"

Eli gave her an apologetic look, then rubbed his hand over Scotty's cap. "Oh, I used to watch that television show

'*MacGyver*' when I was growing up. Learned a few tricks from that and from experimenting on my own with things."

Gena snorted her disbelief. "You mean to tell me that you learned how to survive from a television show? You really do live in your own little world, don't you?"

Eli rolled his eyes. "I've tested my tactics thoroughly," he replied. "Most of them work. I mean, with the right conditions." Then for Scotty's sake, he added, "And with an adult present at all times, of course."

"Can you show me how to do that?" Scotty asked, hopeful.

"No, better not. I don't think your mama would approve."

"That is correct," Gena said, shaking her head. "I don't approve of most of what I've seen from you."

Eli shot her an indulgent smile. "And yet, here we are, stuck with each other."

Gena glanced over her shoulder as they hurried toward the farm yard. "Don't remind me." But she smiled after she said it.

He shrugged, then leaned close. "I am not a violent man. I purposely didn't bring any of my own guns to protect the boy, so I had to improvise." He patted the shotgun on his backpack. "And I don't want to use this—it's just a precaution."

She should be grateful for that, at least. He had protected them, using whatever means he had available and as was the CHAIM custom, he hadn't killed anyone yet. Maybe his methods weren't so sound and time-tested, but the three of them were still alive and…together. "Thank you," she said. Then she added, her voice dripping with sarcasm, "For not being a violent man."

He gave her a hard look. "Your tone makes me think you don't believe that."

"I wonder why. But I do appreciate your efforts."

Eli glanced over at her as if he hadn't heard her correctly. "What was that?"

"You know what I'm saying," she replied. "I appreciate everything you've done for us—in spite of your reputation for being a hothead."

He stopped as they reached the edge of the woods, then looked over the yard and house across the way. "That's good, because things will probably get worse before we get to where we're going. And I'll probably turn into a hothead again before it's all over."

"And where exactly *do* you hope we'll wind up when this is all over, Eli?"

He touched a gloved finger to her chin. "As far away from Maine as I can possibly take us."

The little farmhouse was warm and clean. That was all Eli could ask for at this point. He'd made sure everything was secure and so far, no one had followed them out of the woods. But Gena couldn't seem to relax.

"Eat your soup," Eli told Scotty, his eyes moving from his son to Gena. "That goes for you, too."

Gena stirred the steaming chicken soup. "I don't have much of an appetite."

Scotty, in his usual pragmatic way, cut right to the chase. "She's worried about those guys. What if they find us hiding out here?"

Eli lifted his gaze back toward his son. "I circled back when you were getting settled, gave them a new set of tracks to follow. I think they're gone by now. Or at least the one following us this morning is gone."

"Are you sure?" Scotty asked, a cracker in his hand.

How did he answer that? No, he wasn't sure, but he was hoping against hope that he was right. "As sure as a man can be, sitting inside a house that doesn't belong to him."

Scotty slurped his soup. "It's Christmas," he said, his gaze downcast. "We don't have any presents."

Gena's eyes held Eli's. "But we have each other. I know it's been rough on you, honey, but Eli is trying to protect us. We'll celebrate Christmas when…when this is over."

Eli seconded that. "I'll show both of you how to have a good ol' bayou Christmas, complete with a bonfire and lots of joyous celebrations." Then he tapped a finger near Scotty's bowl. "But for now, we're safe and warm and we have a place to stay out of the cold."

"What if we get in trouble, for breaking in?"

Gena glared at Eli. "Yes, how would you handle that?"

"We won't get in trouble because we didn't break in. The lock came open very easily. It's all been taken care of."

"Do you know these people?"

Eli dropped his soup spoon, then cupped his hands on the table. "Not exactly. Let's just say we're borrowing the house and as long as we do no harm, everything should be just fine. We'll leave things exactly as we found them."

"But we ate their soup. Are we gonna leave a tip?"

Eli burst out laughing. "We just might. What a great idea. You are always one step ahead of me, hotshot Scott."

Beaming with pride, Scotty said, "I have a couple of quarters in my pocket."

"Thanks, but I think we should leave a little more than that."

Gena got up and slammed her uneaten soup into the sink. Eli turned to Scotty. "Why don't you go into the den by the fire and watch one of those children's videos we found in the cabinet? I'm gonna help your mama clear the table."

Scotty scooted out of his chair and ran across the arched doorway to the dark-paneled den. Soon the television was blaring with a cartoon.

Eli came up behind Gena at the sink. "He's a good kid."

"Unless he learns from you."

"Ouch." He pushed at her arm. "Hey, I'm trying here, okay. First, I'm not so used to kids, especially when I'm out on the run in the cold woods. And second, I'm walking a thin line between doing my job and protecting both of you and trying to maintain a legal level of intimidation with these people. I don't want to teach him any bad ways, but I have to do what needs to be done to protect him."

She let out a sigh, her gaze scanning the tall pines and birch trees through the blinds in the kitchen window. "I understand that, but I don't like all his questions and the way you have to evade the real answers. He'll keep asking questions. But how long can you keep putting off the answers?"

Eli whirled her around to face him. "As long as it takes to keep him alive. Do you understand that?"

Gena put her hand to her mouth to stifle her reply. "I think I do. And that's your only saving grace right now. I need you for that, if nothing else."

Her words cut through Eli's heart, shredding the little shards of hope he'd held there. Would this woman ever forgive him for coming to find his son? Would she ever forgive him for being alive and bent on being a father to Scotty? Turning sullen, he stared down at her, hoping to hurt her with his retort. "Yes, and right now *your* only saving grace is that you are the only mother that little boy has ever known. So don't make me regret bringing you with me. Because whether you like it or not, I'm taking him to Louisiana where I can keep him safe."

She pushed away from him. "You wouldn't dare take him without me! Not even you could be that cruel, Eli."

"No, I don't want to do that, but if you can't get it inside that pretty head of yours that I'm doing everything in my power to take care of both of you, then you can just call your brother to come and fetch you and let me take care of the rest."

"How about I call my brother to come and get *both* of us, so we can be away from *you?*"

Eli saw the mad in her eyes. It reflected his own pent-up rage. "Do that, *catin,* and you have my promise. I will track you down and no one, not even your brother, will be able to stop me when I do. So you have your choice here. Either accept me and let me get us to safety, or take matters into your own hands and suffer the consequences."

He moved away, his hand slicing through his hair in frustration. Then because he needed some air and some time to think, he grabbed his coat and went out the back door.

But he'd forgotten his cell phone.

Gena saw the silent phone lighting up and quickly grabbed it. "Devon?"

"Gena, what are you doing answering this phone?"

"Eli's outside. I need to talk to you."

"Are you and Scotty all right?"

"We're okay. We're in the farmhouse. But…Devon I need you to just get us out of here. I can't do this. I don't want Eli—"

"What has he done?"

She heard the deadly tone of her brother's question.

Taking a breath, she tried to remember all that Eli had gone through to save them. Devon would send in the whole CHAIM team if he thought otherwise. "He's done everything right, but…I just need to get Scotty out of this mess. And I don't know how. Devon, I've always known what to do, but this is way out of my league."

Her brother let out a long sigh. "Listen, I know Eli can be hard to live with and believe me, I'd like nothing more than to come and get you. But…technically…I'm retired from CHAIM. I can only do so much. I had to pull out all the stops to get people out there to find Eli's truck. The higher-ups don't believe all his theories as it is—they think he's still a little too paranoid. And if I come up there, it will only bring attention to you and it could endanger Lydia, too. I won't risk that again. Right now, Eli is the agent in charge and…well…you just have to do as he tells you. I trust him because I know he loves Scotty. And in spite of his brusque nature, he wouldn't hurt you, either."

"But he hates me," she said, whirling as she heard the kitchen door open.

Eli saw Gena holding his phone and stomped across the room to grab it. "Devon?"

"I see your charm is still intact," Devon said. "What have you done to upset my sister so much?"

"Did she call you?" Eli asked, giving Gena a dark frown. She crossed her arms over her stomach, glaring right back at him.

"No, I called and she answered. You're losing your grip, Eli."

"I was distracted by someone's constant whining in my ear. Your sister doesn't trust me. She hates me." He stared straight at Gena, daring her to deny that. She looked sheepish, but she stayed silent.

"Funny, she thinks *you* hate her. Can you two possibly put your differences aside to protect Scotty?"

"*Oui*, bro. I'm more than willing to comply. But your stubborn sister seems determined to undermine me at every turn."

Devon actually chuckled. "I think I can feel the sparks all the way down to Georgia. Have you finally met your match?"

"I'm in way over my head, yes. But I'm determined to make her see things my way."

"With that wonderful charm, no doubt."

"I've been known to sweet-talk a woman now and then, *tu comprends*." He winked at Gena when he said that, but she turned away with a derisive groan.

"And you've also been known to railroad people." Devon sighed. "Listen, this is fascinating, but Lydia's mother has a pot roast waiting and we've got a wedding to plan and I'm trying to keep from leaving all of that to come up there myself. I just wanted to tell you that your truck is hidden about a mile from the farmhouse in some dense woods." He gave Eli the coordinates. "Wait until dark and go to the truck and get out of Maine. Tonight. And take care of my sister and…Scotty. I mean that, Eli. Don't let me down on this."

"You don't have to tell me twice," Eli replied, his eyes still on Gena.

"Good. I've done all I can do for now. The higher-ups are not happy with your little vacation."

"Since when have they ever been pleased with me?"

"True. But just so you know, they'll probably put an extra GPS on your fancy truck. So they can track you."

Eli grunted, then said, "And just so you know, I intend to disarm that GPS as soon as I get to my truck. Because, bro, where we're going, they don't need to know."

"And where exactly are you going?"

Eli grinned. "You don't need to know that either."

Then he clicked his phone shut, his grin still intact as he stared at Gena. "Well, big brother seems to think the best place for you and the boy is with me, *chère*. Make the best of it."

Gena shot him an ugly look, then hurried into the den to Scotty.

Eli told himself he didn't care how she felt about him as long as he got Scotty to safety. He told himself that even while his heart hurt from the pain of her disapproval. And even while his memories of holding her were as vanilla-scented as a magnolia blossom and as warm with promise as a bayou dawn.

He stared out the window, then mumbled, "For sure, I hate the cold."

ELEVEN

Eli itched to be on the move again. Since their earlier disagreement, he and Gena hadn't spoken to each other unless it had been absolutely necessary. At least her silent treatment had given him a few precious hours to talk to his son.

His son. That phrase always jarred him. He both loved it and feared it. But Scotty was so amazing, each minute with the little boy was like a precious gift. A very precious gift from God—the best Christmas present.

Lydia would be proud, Eli thought as he once again stuffed his backpack full of supplies, then went over the mental list of everything he needed to do. If he could just get back to Louisiana, he'd be on solid ground again. He'd be able to sit down and figure out this thing. He opened the survival kit, touched a hand to Scotty's picture, then slammed it shut again.

"It's time to go," he said as he turned to Gena. They'd found some children's books in a basket by the fireplace and now Scotty was reading the story of the birth of Christ out loud to his mother. A normal scene—warm and cozy on most winter nights—but not tonight.

Gena glanced up at him, her gaze hinting at remorse.

But just hinting. She wasn't ready to call a truce with him. And could he blame her? He'd never been one for sweet words and gentle gestures. How many times had he been told that he was hard-hearted and cruel?

Too many. Except for Leah. Leah had seen right through him, had tamed him, made him want to be a better man. But his grandfather and CHAIM had changed that notion. And Leah's death had only hardened his cold heart even more.

Don't let your heart turn to mush now, he told himself. Don't give in to that need. It would hurt too much. Way too much. He had to save his heart for his son. And that meant he'd have to forget about Gena. Get her to safety, get your son to safety. Then worry about the rest.

Gena bundled Scotty into his coat and hat. "All ready?"

Scotty nodded. "Where are we going now?"

She looked up at Eli. "I'm not sure. But soon, we'll be back home."

"To have our Christmas," Scotty replied.

Eli squatted in front of his son. "Remember this afternoon when I told you all about Christmas back in Louisiana? It'll more than make up for this."

"Is that where we're going?" Gena asked, coiling her wool scarf around her neck.

Eli eyed her for signs of disapproval. "I can keep both of you safe there." He stood up. "And I do mean both of you."

He saw relief and regret instead. "Eli, I—"

Before she could finish, they heard a motor revving and the squeal of tires as a vehicle whirled right up to the back door.

"Stay here!" Eli hit the window, a finger slitting the blinds. "That's my truck."

Before he could get to the door, a hulking figure rushed up the steps, then began beating on the wood. "Eli, open up. Now!"

Eli groaned. He knew that voice. "What are you doing here, Whelan?"

"I'll explain later," came the lilting Irish brogue. "Let me in!"

Eli motioned to Gena, then unlocked the door, opening it wide enough to reach out his hand. Grabbing the man by the collar of his fur-lined coat, Eli hauled him close. "*Oui*, for sure you have some explaining to do, Shepherd. Starting with what you're doing here."

The man facing him laughed out loud. "Well, Disciple, I'd say we have a lot to catch up on. And it's a wee bit cold out here, so please let a *bráthier* in."

Eli released the man, then yanked him through the door. "First, you're not my brother. And second, talk fast because you do not want to get on my last nerve."

The man waved to Gena and Scotty. "Hello, I'm Brice Whelan, better known as the Shepherd."

Gena nodded. "Hello. What's going on?"

Brice grinned at her blunt question. "Devon warned me about her," he said to Eli. "Hear you've just about got your hands full."

Eli backed him against the wall. "Talk, Brice. Right now."

Brice sighed. "Relax, will you? CHAIM sent me to help you out of this sorry mess. Just load up and get in the truck and we'll be on our way. I'll explain everything. Time is of the utmost importance, understand?"

Eli lifted his backpack, then motioned for Gena. "Fine, but I'm driving." Then he turned, a finger in the man's face. "And don't try anything, Brice, or I'll dump you on the side of the road and leave you to freeze solid. I've had just about enough for one day."

Brice chuckled again, brushing at his burnished golden-brown hair. "Devon said you were doing battle with several bad men and one pretty determined woman." He shot Gena a charming Irish smile.

Gena stared him down, then glared at Eli. "Great. Two of you now. Can we just get out of here?"

"That's exactly why I'm here."

Brice bowed, all flourish and manners, while Eli silently promised to throttle Devon Malone next time he saw him. "We didn't need any help."

Brice followed him to the truck. "Devon thought you did. And *we* didn't feel the need to ask how you felt about it."

"Some things never change." Eli helped Gena in the tiny back seat, then lifted Scotty up beside her. "We'll discuss this later," he told Brice.

"Who's he?" Scotty asked, clearly fascinated with Brice.

Eli and Brice got in the truck, Eli at the wheel. Then he turned to his son. "Him? He's a…coworker who runs a very…uh…nice retreat in Ireland. I lived there for a while."

Brice grinned. "Ah, those were the days, weren't they now?"

"Don't remind me," Eli said under his breath.

"Well, behave and you won't have to…visit again," Brice countered.

Scotty leaned forward. "You mean if you get in trouble, you have to go there for a time-out?"

"The lad's very smart," Brice said, slapping his knee.

Eli glared at him as he eased the truck out into the night. "Brice lives in a big castle by the sea. He runs the place. He gets a lot of visitors."

"Tired visitors," Brice added. "Visitors who need a good long rest in a peaceful secure place."

"A castle with swords and knights and everything? I'd like to see that," Scotty replied.

"Maybe one day you and your mother could come and visit Ireland. It's a lovely land, but I'm afraid we don't have knights in armor. Just regular men and women."

Gena touched a hand to Scotty's arm. "No more questions right now. Let them do their jobs, honey."

Scotty sat silent for a minute, then said, "What kind of jobs are you guys doing, anyway?"

Eli shot Brice a warning glance. Brice shrugged. "Search and rescue, business development, research and marketing analysis, rebuilding, restoring, helping other people. Whatever is needed."

"Shh," Gena said when Scotty opened his mouth to ask yet another question. "Rest, honey. We've got a long way to go."

"Aye, that we have, indeed," Brice replied.

The truck roared along until they'd reached a major interstate and were headed south.

"*We* won't be going all the way on this trip," Eli told Brice. "That is, *you* won't be going along for the entire trip."

"How's that?" Brice countered. "You're really gonna throw me out?"

"I just might."

Brice held a hand to his heart. "You pain me. I just got here."

"Just tell me the plan," Eli said in a hiss. "And then I'll decide what to do with you."

Brice hooted with laughter again. "Still got that biting sense of humor, I see."

Eli didn't smile. "You still smell like sheep, I see."

"Do not. I bought new clothes just for America. And I had a nice warm shower with olive oil soap this morning."

"Once a shepherd…"

"Now you're just being downright mean."

Eli cut his eyes to his so-called friend and fellow agent. "And don't you forget it."

Gena wasn't sure whether to shout for joy or wail like a baby. Apparently, because her brother couldn't come to her rescue and because neither Devon nor she could truly trust Eli, Devon had called in reinforcements. Brice Whelan was the exact opposite of Eli Trudeau. He was friendly, full of mirth and very open to talking about things when he wasn't quoting poets and reciting Shakespeare.

Eli had gone back into his brute-force commando mode—that same mode her brother and her deceased husband had both used at times. Only Eli brought it to a new level with his grunts and his code talk.

Trying to remember what Devon had told her about Brice, she thought back over the little bit of information she'd learned on the need-to-know basis about Devon's CHAIM team over the years. She knew there were about five or six of them—Richard's code name had been the Lion, probably because of his golden-blond hair and his big-boned athletic frame. Richard had always reminded her of a Viking, come to conquer her. And she'd fallen for him hard.

Then there was her brother, Devon, who had that puzzling pastoral code name that everyone bemoaned. Yet it suited him. He was as still and steady as a country landscape at times. At other times, just like a landscape, he changed to become fast-moving and wild.

Then there was Kissie—the Woman at the Well—who

lived and worked in New Orleans where CHAIM kept a safe house.

And now here was Brice—the Irishman who did indeed live in a big castle, at least part of the time. He had an American mother who lived in Atlanta and a base of operations there for his American enterprises. From what she remembered, the Shepherd really was a shepherd. He owned a sheep farm and worked hard as overseer of a big operation in County Kilkenny that produced some of the finest Irish wool in the world. Single, as were most of the team members when they'd started out, and just like the other members, he traveled all over the world to help Christians in need.

Did he think she was in need? Or had he come here to make sure Eli didn't do anything he'd regret?

Right now, they were talking in code, so it was hard to tell what was going on in the front seat of the big double-cab truck. Scotty was asleep, so Gena leaned forward to hear more. Brice had quoted from *Exodus,* something about judgment.

"'You shall put in the breast-piece of judgment.'"

Eli shook his head. "So I am being called forth to pay for my sins? Is that what you're trying to tell me, Shepherd?"

Brice lowered his voice. "'But you were full of judgment on the wicked; Judgment and justice take hold of you.'"

Gena had enough. Slapping the back of the seat, she made sure Scotty was asleep then said, "Okay, I get *Exodus* and *Job* references, and I know all about how you guys talk in Bible code. Eli, he's trying to tell you that you once judged someone too harshly and now someone is coming after you with their own judgment. Am I right?"

Brice turned, mouth open, his head moving in confirmation.

Eli was more vocal. "*Oui*, tell me something I don't know already. I tried to warn everyone. That's why I came to this frozen tundra in the first place. I had to see for myself if the boy was safe."

Brice turned toward Eli. "And that's why I'm here. You *were* right. Between Devon and Kissie and myself, we've managed to piece together a bit of information."

"And that is?"

Brice leaned back in his seat. "It does stem from that mess down in Rio Branco—"

Eli hit the steering wheel so hard that Gena jumped. "Will that episode haunt me for the rest of my days?"

"Probably," Brice said, his tone practical and sure. "Can I finish?"

"Go on."

Brice lowered his voice, but Gena could still hear him. "Your grandfather had some very wealthy cult members from all over the world. Some of them not too happy that we managed to bust up the cult and end things and some of them are still angry that their family members got caught up in such a vile operation."

"So you think someone is coming after me—after Scotty—for one of those reasons?" Eli whispered.

Gena heard the implication of Eli's question and re-membered Eli's version of the same conclusion. Someone wanted to take Scotty—Eli's son—in order to get back at him. But who and why?

"Why would taking Scotty make things right?"

She didn't realize she'd said that out loud until the truck became silent and she looked up to find Brice staring at her and Eli's gaze on her in the rearview mirror. At least she hadn't woken up her son.

Brice didn't answer. He just looked over at Eli.

Eli let out a sigh, then said, "An eye for an eye."

Gena's heart fluttered in fear, recoiling from what Eli had already tried to tell her. "So this isn't about some drug operation getting back on track. This is about revenge, pure and simple?"

Eli nodded. "*Oui,* could be. But not so pure and surely not so very simple. Whoever this is thinks I caused everything to fall apart. And as I've said over and over, I have reason to believe my grandfather Savoy got this ball rolling before he ever left this earth. He might have set up someone to take over if anything happened to him. And their first line of business—to make me suffer in the worst possible way."

"That's one theory," Brice said. "Or...this could be someone still angry with the whole cult. And because it is no more, and because the Peacemaker has met his maker, that leaves Eli holding the bag, so to speak."

Gena tried to draw a breath, but her throat muscles refused to cooperate. "That's what you kept telling me." She looked over at Brice. "So you came all this way just to confirm what Eli already knew?"

"I suppose I did, yes. And to offer my help." Brice looked over at Eli. "Because in spite of his surly nature and his denial of needing any help, I grew very fond of the Disciple during our time together. And because I know he'd do the same thing if he were in my shoes."

"Don't be so sure," Eli replied.

But his words were gentle this time and full of what Gena could only recognize as appreciation.

"What can we do?" she asked, refusing to think past the here and now, her eyes on her sleeping son.

Eli lifted his head. "We go to Louisiana so I can go

through my grandfather's records and hopefully find a clue that will help us decide who's so intent on taking my son."

Gena had to ask the next question, although just as with everything else they'd discussed, she was pretty sure she knew the answer. "And what will you do when you find this person?"

Eli's dark look shot through the mirror as the interstate lights flashed past them. His answer was calm, deadly calm. "I intend to stop this person, of course. You have my word on that."

Gena believed him. But at what cost? Eli was the kind of man who'd fight to the finish, CHAIM rules and regulations aside. He didn't like following the rules.

And right now, Gena couldn't help herself. She was glad he was that kind of man. For her son's sake, at least.

TWELVE

Brice's hand cut through the air. "I haven't told you the good and bad of things."

Eli shifted in his seat, wondering what other surprises the Shepherd had up his sleeve. "You mean, there's more?"

"Well, yes. I didn't come all this way just to hear you say you told us so, brother."

Eli didn't need a grim reminder of how he'd tried to warn CHAIM about his bad feeling and he didn't want any more surprises. "Talk."

"The good news, I have a plan. I can get you to a private jet. Much quicker for travel in this weather than your truck, don't you think?" He held up the weatherproof CHAIM GPS tracker Eli had found underneath the truck's frame, then threw it out the window. "And much harder to track because I have my plane swept for bugs before every flight."

Eli smiled for the very first time. "Good idea. And where is this private jet? And who exactly will be waiting for us on the tarmac?"

"No one. I didn't give you up, Eli. I might be tough as a retreat manager and interrogator, but I'm on your side here. So as far as they know, *I'm* tracking you and I'm supposed to report back. But I don't have to do that right away, now, do I? I happen to own a company jet—Whelan Wool has offices all over the world, you know."

"*Oui,* I know all about your little operation. I also know you're an expert negotiator. Is that the real reason you're here? Do you think I've taken these two hostage?"

Brice looked sheepish. "Just a guise to get here, brother. Nothing more. I told CHAIM I might be able to talk you down from whatever far-fetched plan you had in mind."

"No such luck," Eli replied.

Gena chimed right in. "Does CHAIM think Scotty and I are hostages?"

Brice lifted a hand to halt her. "They have concerns, yes. But your brother has tried to assure everyone involved that Eli did not take you hostage. In fact, that's why Devon called *me*—to hold them off until I can report. And in the meantime, we'll get you to safety—no one will know where you are unless you want them to know."

"Like I believe that."

He gave Eli a look that begged for trust. "Eli, I was there last time, remember? I know what you went through."

"Is this your way of trying to make nice to me now, *mon ami?*"

Brice let out a grunt of frustration. "You are not a forgiving man, but yes, I'd like to make amends."

"And you're willing to loan me a jet just like that, no questions asked?"

"No questions asked, as long as you do your best to get to the bottom of this and as long as you protect Devon's sister and her son, of course."

Eli nodded. "Agreed."

"Okay, then. We need to make it to New York and to JFK. I'll call ahead and get clearance."

Eli pushed at the steering wheel. "Don't do that just yet. I need to think."

Eli wasn't used to giving over his trust, especially to Brice. Brice had been a tough taskmaster back in Ireland, always hovering, always on guard, always around, trying to use his skills on Eli so he'd break and open up. But Brice had been fair, and if Eli were perfectly honest, he knew Brice had been trying to help him find his way back to reality. But then, Eli hated every memory of those dark days of isolation, including all the people who'd tried to help him.

"Eli?"

He felt Gena's hand on his shoulder. *"Oui?"*

"I think we should take Brice up on his offer. Scotty can't keep up like this and neither can I. If getting on a plane can make this trip easier and quicker and help us to end this nightmare, then I'm all for it."

Brice shot Eli a triumphant grin. "Devon said she was smart and capable. Can't argue with that kind of logic."

Eli tried to find an argument, but he had the boy to consider. He let out a breath. "Okay. Brice, do what you can to make it happen."

Brice pulled out a phone and started punching instructions. But Eli grabbed his arm. "And just remember, if you're setting me up, you will live to regret it."

Brice pulled away. "I'm not setting you up, Eli. I want you to find some peace in your life."

Eli wanted that, too, but he had a bad feeling peace would be a long time coming.

Gena touched his shoulder again. "Thank you."

Eli grunted to hide how her feather-like touch made his heart beat go up in tempo. "You can thank me later, when I know for sure Scotty's safe."

The truck grew silent again. When Eli glanced back in the mirror, Gena had pulled Scotty into her arms and closed her eyes. Good. She needed to sleep. Eli's own fatigue dragged like a heavy anchor through him, but sleep was the last thing on his mind. He was too keyed up.

His grandfather, no doubt, had a long list of powerful, vengeful friends, left to do his bidding and left to either run and hide or try and salvage what the CHAIM team had destroyed. And Eli wouldn't sleep until he'd covered every name on that list. But first, he had to find all of his grandfather's hidden files. And purge the rest of the Peacemaker's secrets.

Gena watched as Brice and Eli went over the flight plan. Again. These two were very thorough. And that was a good thing for her and Scotty.

"I can't believe we get to fly in a plane," Scotty said. "I've never done that."

"I know," Gena said. "We haven't gone on very many trips." And that was on purpose. They'd always had plenty to keep them occupied right there in their little cove.

"It's big," Scotty said as they waited inside a small glass-enclosed room just off the tarmac.

Gena glanced out at the sleek jet. "Yes, it sure is. Very impressive."

The double-W crest on the side of the jet looked majestic and first-class, while Brice Whelan looked anything but. The man was as rugged as they came, all brawn and shaggy hair and shining golden-green eyes. And Eli looked as out of place beside the expensive plane as a trapper next to a Southern mansion.

"Give me strength," she said, her prayer moving on a continuous loop.

She watched as the two men came inside, still discussing. "Are we ready?"

Brice rolled his eyes. "Yes, we've been ready. But Mr. Trudeau here had to go over the flight check for the third time. And intimidate my crew while he was doing it."

"Trust but verify," Eli retorted. "I wanted to make sure the crew did a thorough safety check."

"My crew is the best in the business," Brice said. "And I've had all of them checked out several times over. There are no enemies here, Eli. Now you need to get on that plane."

Eli ran a hand over his tousled hair. "Okay, all right. I'm just antsy."

Brice inclined his head. "We all are that. But…if it makes you feel any better, I'll be flying the plane."

Eli leveled him with a frown. "Really? You failed to mention that. Why is that?"

Brice poked a finger at Eli's down jacket. "Because I knew you'd resist that notion. I'm going with you, Eli. That's the only way you'll get on my plane."

Eli hit a hand against the heavy glass window. "I should have known there was a catch."

"No catch. Just a precaution."

Eli looked from Brice to Gena. She could see the doubt and distrust in his eyes. She stared at Brice, sizing him up. "You promised us—"

"I promised you I'd get you away and that I wouldn't report back to CHAIM. And I will keep that promise. But I need to be on that plane with you. That's the deal."

Gena stood up. "Eli, let's just go."

Eli paced back and forth for a couple of minutes. "Okay. But we need to land somewhere where no one will be expecting us. Can you do that?"

"I'm the pilot," Brice replied. "Don't worry, I know how to fly the plane and I have a very good copilot. Where do you want to go?"

"Let's land her upstate," Eli said, nodding. "That way we can take a car the rest of the way." Mimicking Brice's earlier words, he added, "*Just as a precaution.*"

"Upstate it is," Brice replied. "Shreveport? Alexandria? Monroe?"

Eli looked surprised. "I see you've studied up on Louisiana."

"Part of the job, Eli."

Gena held her breath, wondering if Eli would grab them both up and bolt off this airstrip.

"Alex," he said, nodding. "Middle of the state, more north than south. I can get us the rest of the way."

"Deal," Brice replied. "And I can evade until you're where you want to be."

"Let's go." Eli reached for Gena. "How are you doing?"

"I've been better. But Scotty's excited about getting on a plane, at least."

Eli scooped the grinning little boy up into his arms. "Is that right? Think you might get to help Brice fly?"

"Can I?"

Brice grinned back at him. "We can arrange that, maybe. We're in luck. It's a clear night."

Scotty giggled as Eli pulled Gena along and started toward the waiting plane. Eli turned at the door, giving Gena a look that told her to hang on.

She did, her hand touching on his jacket as they walked across the cold tarmac and up the steps to the open door. Once they were inside, Gena noted the plush interior, then settled Scotty into his seat. After meeting the steward named Roderick, she turned to Eli. "We're not going to have to parachute out or anything like that, are we?"

Eli put a hand up against the beige leather seat, blocking her, his dark gaze too close. "No, we're not going to have to do that."

Gena grabbed his arm—she seemed to be doing that a lot lately. "Eli, you did check this jet out completely, right?"

He put his hand on hers, then held it between them. "You know I did, *chère*. I wouldn't put the boy on this plane if I didn't believe it's safe."

"Good." She pulled away, but he held her hand tight in his. "Are we okay, you and me?"

The message in his gaze was unmistakable. He wanted her to trust him. Gena swallowed, nodded. "I'm sorry about...back at the farmhouse. It's just been hard."

"I know, I know." He pulled her close for just a minute, his lips grazing her forehead. "Hopefully, it'll all be over soon and then we can figure out...how to handle everything else."

Gena's cold, numb mind registered that brief bit of warmth as his lips touched her skin. It gave her hope. She looked up at him, her smile weak. "Thank you."

Then she turned to find her son and Brice watching them. Scotty didn't say anything, but his confused look brought Gena out of her warm and fuzzy feeling, reminding her that she had to tread lightly with her heart here.

Brice walked by, then dropped his voice. "No hostage

situation here. At least I can report back truthfully on that account."

Eli stepped away. "What do you mean?"

Brice stood between them, his mirthful gaze moving from Gena to Eli. "What I mean, brother, is that the woman seems more than willing to follow you anywhere in the world, and I don't think it's the Stockholm syndrome at work."

"Only because right now, she has no other choice," Eli said loud enough for Gena to hear him.

Gena sank down in her seat next to Scotty, her mind reeling with all sorts of revelations as she fastened her seat belt and made sure Scotty knew how to fasten his. She didn't want to be here, in this situation. And earlier today, she'd wanted nothing more than to be rescued and away from Eli and all that he'd brought to her door. But somehow, listening to him talk to Brice inside the car, she'd managed to understand that Eli was a man who'd suffered at the hands of his own flesh and blood. And he'd paid for his past sins, dearly paid. He'd lost his wife and his son. Now he had a chance to redeem himself, with his son at least. He'd gone from that "eye for an eye" principle to asking for God's grace in his life. How could she fault him for wanting that?

No, she didn't want to be on the run from dangerous people. She didn't want her son to be a target of some person out for vengeance. But…she had to admit, she wanted to be near Eli Trudeau. And not because she didn't have a choice. But because he was her child's father and because she was beginning to have strong feelings for the gentle man buried underneath that cold, dark heart.

Which meant that now she wasn't just concerned about her little boy. She was also very concerned about his father. And she'd do whatever it took to keep *both* of them alive.

THIRTEEN

Eli had to hand it to the Shepherd. In spite of looking like a sheepherder most days, Brice Whelan had the best of everything money could buy, even good employees. The copilot appeared well-qualified and loyal. And even though Eli didn't like the skinny, skittish steward's hovering, Roderick was always Johnny-on-the-spot with anything that could make them comfortable. Brice's equipment was state-of-the-art from his fancy plane to the laptop he'd provided for Eli to his many smart phones and other gadgets. This plane was a flying spy ship and Eli was using that to his full advantage to do research on both his grandfather and anything or anybody else connected to Rio Branco.

"Whatcha doing?"

He looked up from studying some archived files to find his son staring at him. Obviously, Scotty was as fascinated with computers as his mother. Gena had already drooled over Brice's equipment, marking it as very high-tech and high-cost. "I'm working," Eli said for lack of a better explanation. "Studying some files, catching up on some important articles. What are you doing?"

Scotty shrugged. "I can't sleep. I'm bored."

Eli laughed at that. "Where's Mom?"

Scotty pointed to the double seat behind Eli. "She's tired. I didn't want to wake her up."

Glad to hear that Gena was finally resting, Eli patted the seat next to him. "C'mon over here and we'll find a game to play on that big-screen television."

That brought a gleam to Scotty's eyes. "I love video games, but Mom lets me play them only after I've done my school work." He scooted next to Eli, then looked up at him. "Am I going back to school?"

Eli's heart seemed to shatter into a million silent pieces, each one cutting at his breath like crystallized ice. What could he tell this innocent child? What could he possibly say or do to reassure his son, because he didn't know the outcome of this himself? He wouldn't lie, but he wouldn't let his son down either. "I'm going to do my best to have you back home safe. Do you believe me?"

Scotty bobbed his head. "My mom said you're going to take care of us. She told me to be brave."

Eli had to swallow. He'd stared down dangerous criminals and rebellious factions and he'd overcome personal tragedy, but he wasn't sure how to face the protective, unconditional love he felt as he stared down at his son. This kind of love was indeed worth dying for—a welcome weight. "You are truly brave. And so is your *maman.* I need you to stay brave for me." He leaned close then, eye to eye with Scotty. "I'm going to get us out of this."

Scotty stared back at him, his big brown eyes trusting and luminous. "You know what? I wish you were my father."

Eli sat back in his seat, stunned into silence, tears pricking at his eyes, teeth gritted so tightly his jaw clinched. Wanting with every fiber of his being to take his son up in his arms and tell him the truth, he fought at his frustrations. He couldn't respond.

When he looked up, he saw Roderick standing near the front galley, his eyes on Scotty. Eli didn't like the way the man stared like a scared rabbit. Then he heard a noise behind them and turned to find Gena standing, holding on to the back of his seat, her long hair mussed and her eyes sleep-glazed but shocked open.

Her gaze moved from her son to Eli. "What's going on?"

Scotty got up on his knees in his seat, facing her. "We're gonna play a video game. Is that okay?"

Gena's response was weak with relief. "Yes, honey, that's okay."

Eli stood, making a big deal out of stretching to hide his trembling. "Could I have a word with you?" he asked Gena. Then he told Scotty to pick out a game.

Leading Gena to the back of the plane so no one else could listen, he leaned close. "Did you hear that?"

"Yes." Her whisper was razor-sharp. "We're going to have to explain things to him eventually."

Eli looked down at the carpet. "But not right now. He's confused enough already. Let's wait until—"

"Until this is over," she finished, her eyes locking with his. "Will it ever be over?"

"If I have things my way, yes." Then because he had to know, he asked, "How do you feel about that? About telling him, I mean?"

Her face was shadowed with worry. "I've fought it and my head tells me to fight *you,* but my heart tells me that would be wrong. You came to us when we needed you and for that I'm grateful. I want you to know your son. But we have to do this together. That's the best way for Scotty."

"*Oui,* you won't get an argument from me on that. I won't say anything unless we tell him together. Agreed?"

"Agreed." She lifted her head toward the laptop. "Any results?"

Eli couldn't tell her everything, but he did want to offer her some hope. "I've narrowed the list down to people who are now in jail and people who had family members involved in the cult down there. I'm thinking it has to be someone who resents our breaking up the cult. All the drug-runners have scattered and none of them would have the resources to come after CHAIM. But some of the cult members had very powerful family connection both down there and here in the States. Maybe one of them is out for revenge." He shrugged. "These were mostly young people, disgruntled and searching. They were vulnerable to both the drugs and to the organization's charismatic persuasions. Some of them might be bitter that they lost what they considered a family and now they're out to prove a point, or maybe hoping to revive the entire operation."

"But why? You'd think they'd be glad to be out of that place."

"Drugs and false hope are very powerful tools, *chère.* It's not that easy to debrief someone who's been brainwashed. Especially if that someone had a vested interest in this kind of thing."

Gena shuddered, causing Eli's protective instincts to kick in. He reached for her to steady her and just as he did, the plane hit some turbulence, bringing her right into his arms.

"Steady," he said, so close he could smell the apple scent of her hair. Because she was warm and because she wasn't pushing him away, he held her there, reveling in the security he felt each time he touched her. Gena was becoming a lifeline for him—a lifeline to his son and to the kind of life he'd been cheated of so far. Eli wanted to hold on with all his strength, but he was afraid to do that.

Gena looked up at him, her eyes reflecting his thoughts from the way she drank him in. He leaned closer.

"Hey, Mr. Eli, I'm ready!"

Scotty's impatient shout brought them apart. He touched a finger to her nose. "One day, you and I are going to have some alone time. We deserve that much at least."

Gena smiled up at him. "We do?"

"I think so. I liked kissing you. I intend to do it again."

Her smile was soft with longing. "Is that a promise?"

"Yes, and I don't give out promises easily."

She pushed him toward her son. "Well, good, because I don't give out kisses easily."

"I'll keep that in mind," he told her as he moved up the wide aisle toward his seat. But before he sat down, he turned and winked at her. "Right now a kiss and a promise is about all we have to go on."

A kiss and a promise.

Gena wondered how her hopes had become reduced to that. She'd never before lived on promises and kisses... well, it had been a long time since she'd even thought about kissing another man. Somehow, she felt as if she were betraying Richard.

But he's gone, she told herself. He'd want her to get on with things. And he didn't have a chance to know Scotty. They'd never had a chance to have children even though they'd talked about it a lot. Leaning back in her seat now as the plane prepared for its descent, Gena thought about Eli. What would it be like to have a child with him? To have him as a part of her life for a long time to come?

Slow down, she thought, wishing she could just erase these confusing, overwhelming feelings. Maybe she was substituting sympathy for any true romantic feelings she might have for Eli. But remembering their one kiss didn't make her feel any sympathy. It only made her want to get to know him better, to figure out his complex nature and to help him find some salvation again.

Gena closed her eyes, hoping to hide what Eli might see there. Listening to him talk and laugh with Scotty seemed to soothe all her worries. For a man who'd been billed as cold and calculating, he sure knew how to be warm and personable with children. Or at least this child. His child. Her child. It was all so muddled inside her tired brain.

Gena kept her eyes closed for the next few minutes, but Brice's distinguished voice coming over the intercom brought her out of her near-slumber. He explained they'd be landing soon in Alexandria, Louisiana, and that wee-hour weather was an almost balmy fifty-five degrees. "A nice warm spell for a change," he added before he signed off.

She heard Eli's exclamation. "Good. No more snow."

"No snow?" Scotty seemed disappointed, then quickly added, "I guess that's okay because I lost my skates."

"We'll get you new skates," Eli assured him. "Although I don't know how you'll play hockey down here unless we find an indoor rink."

"That would work."

Eli instructed Scotty to fasten his seat belt, then looked over at Gena. "You, too."

"I'm already fastened," she said, her words caught between hope and defeat.

"At least we had an uneventful flight," Eli said, the relief evident in his voice.

Gena thanked God for that. But what would they find once they landed, she had to wonder.

What they found was trouble.

Brice taxied the plane along the private airstrip with expert precision, headed for a private hangar at the end of the woods. Then his voice echoed over the intercom. "So far, so good. Plan to depart immediately, so we can get you on your way."

Eli gathered his equipment and the few other things they'd managed to bring along. "I rented us an SUV online," he told Gena. "It should be waiting at the airport." He'd used one of the code names Brice had been issued, so no one could connect the car to him.

Roderick, the steward, had stayed out of Eli's way so far, but now he came and whispered into Eli's ear. "Mr. Whelan would like a word with you, sir."

Eli entered the cockpit and leaned over Brice and the copilot to stare out into the early morning light. It was still too dark to see anything but trees and heavy foliage. "What's up?"

"Several unauthorized vehicles," Brice retorted. "When I radioed the control tower, they informed me that our escort convoy was waiting. Only I didn't order any escorts. According to airport security, they arrived about fifteen minutes ago and had all the right credentials, so they were allowed into one of the hangars. Several men exited the trucks and now they're nowhere to be found. Which means they're probably waiting for us all right—an ambush of some sort."

"Take her back up," Eli demanded, his eyes still scanning the dark airstrip, his instincts on full-alert. The woods and dense swamp looked still and quiet. Too still and too quiet.

Brice shook his head. "It's too late to get back in the air. They'd probably try to blow up the plane." He shot a look back toward the cabin. "We can't let that happen."

"So…we have to evade them," Eli said, his mind clicking into overdrive. "Or just run them down."

"With the plane?" Brice asked, lifting his dark brows. "First, that would bring attention to us and we'd have the whole airport authority on us. And second, this mysterious team will have guns, Eli. Big guns would be my guess. And even though the plane is built to withstand bullets, I won't risk the boy or Gena getting hurt until we have a better handle on this situation."

Vern, the burly copilot, spoke. "The plane's tough, but a blast could damage the exterior. We could stop here, sir, and let them come to us instead." He grinned up at Eli. "*Then* we could mow them down."

Eli suddenly took a firm liking to Vern. "Good idea."

Brice looked from one to the other, his eyes bright. "Well, stopping here instead of down there would give us time to maybe get the boy out of the plane at least."

Eli squinted into the murky dawn. He envisioned an army of men lurking at the end of the runway, all dressed in dark clothing like a pack of ninjas just waiting to pounce. Whoever was there was very bold, that was for sure.

"How'd they know?" he wondered out loud. "And why aren't they doing a better job of hiding? You'd think they'd just bid their time until we were on the ground."

Brice shook his head. "I have no idea. This plane was

as clean as a hospital operating room. No way they could have bugged us. If they're trying to pose as CHAIM agents, they're doing a lousy job of it."

"What did airport security say?"

"Said the men had official Whelan credentials, so they let them pass. But then they wouldn't have shared anything with security even if they'd been detained. Somehow, they found a way in because they knew we'd be landing here."

"Then someone on this plane had to have alerted them," Eli said. He glanced toward the copilot. "What about your friend here?"

The other man, busy with his work, only grunted. He was efficient and not much of a talker from what Eli had garnered. But that didn't make him trustworthy even if he had suggested they stop here and try to figure a way out.

Brice let out a hoot of laughter. "Vern? He's as gentle as a lamb, but as lethal as a lion. He's my right-hand man, Eli, and a highly trained bodyguard to boot. I'd trust him and my other employees to the ends of the earth."

Eli nodded. "*Oui*, that's a good thing my friend. 'Cause that's where you're gonna need to take this plane. We're not going out into this mess of an ambush to be slaughtered."

Brice gave him a look of disbelief. "You're going to hijack my plane and force me to take you somewhere else?"

"If I have to, yes." He leaned close again. "What about that squirrelly steward? He's been hovering since we took off."

Brice kept his eyes on the airstrip. "That's what stewards do. But just in case, why don't you go and talk to him?"

Eli nodded. "I will do just that."

He turned back toward the cabin to search for the man Brice had assured him he could trust. But Roderick was nowhere to be found. And neither were Gena nor Scotty.

FOURTEEN

Eli ran through the plane, calling Gena's name as a river of adrenaline rushed through his system. When he hit the door of the small galley in the back, his breath froze inside his chest. Roderick stood hunched against the storage cabinets and he had a gun positioned at Gena's temple.

Eli's gaze slammed into Gena's.

"Eli?" she called, waiting.

His name shook on her lips, but she had a determined glint in her eyes. She wouldn't go down without a fight. And that scared him even more than seeing a gun aimed at her head.

"Where's Scotty?" Eli asked, glaring at Roderick.

"That's what I'm waiting to hear," Roderick said, pushing the gun closer to Gena's head. "She got in the way!"

"I told Scotty to hide," Gena said. "Eli, don't let him hurt Scotty."

"You know I won't let that happen." He took a deep breath. "Roderick, what are you trying to accomplish?"

"I need to get that boy off this plane," Roderick said. "They're waiting down there for me."

"Who's waiting?"

"I can't tell you that," Roderick said, his hand shaking.

The kid was as nervous as a cornered cat. "You need to find the boy. Don't make me hurt her."

Eli sized up the situation. This young man was too raw and jittery to be trained in any type of hostage-taking. Someone had probably threatened him or bribed him to do this. Which would explain how he passed all their security checks. Putting on a calm, controlled facade, Eli brushed at his hair. "You know, this is the fourth time in about a week someone has threatened my family. I've had enough."

Roderick didn't know how to respond to that, but the look in Gena's eyes told Eli that she considered him her family, too. Well, he wanted to keep it that way.

"Just get the little boy," Roderick shouted. "I have to do this."

Eli nodded, sensing desperation in Roderick's words. "I'll look for him." He shot Gena a warning look, then ran back to the cockpit as Brice was taxiing the plane around to the long runaway. "We have to get back into the air, Brice. Your trusty steward has a gun on Gena and Scotty is hiding somewhere. It's a setup to take the boy."

Brice hit his hand on the yoke. "This can't be happening. Roderick?"

"*Oui*, Roderick. I think someone forced him because he's not acting like a hit man—more scared and unsure. And I've got to get back before he does something stupid."

Brice kept the plane taxiing. "It's tricky, but I might be able to swing her around with minimal damage." Then he looked up at Eli. "They won't shoot the plane if they know Roderick still has the boy."

"It's our only chance. You figure out how to get the plane back in the air while I stall the kid. Oh, and Brice, if Roderick survives, I highly suggest you fire him."

Brice grunted, then radioed the tower. Turning quickly toward Eli, he said, "Okay. Be careful. We're about to do a one-eighty turn and the takeoff won't be pretty. That should help you distract Roderick and confuse our visitors enough to stall them for a couple of minutes, but we have to either get this plane back in the air or exit to the swamps."

"Take her back up. It's the only way," Eli said, wishing he could take matters into his own hands. "If I didn't have them to worry about—" But then he wouldn't be on this plane if he wasn't trying to protect Gena and Scotty.

"Hey, I'm waiting!"

He turned toward Roderick's shrill shout.

"You need to get back here now," the young man screamed.

"Go," Brice shouted. "Find the boy and hang on to him."

Eli stomped back up the aisle toward where Roderick was still holding Gena. "Gena, do you know where Scotty is?"

She nodded. "But I'm not telling *him*."

Eli gave her a long look, trying to read her silent message and send her one of his own. "But you can tell me, can't you? He might be afraid. Like the night I first came to visit. I was *floored* by your charms that night, remember?"

Gena's eyes locked with his and for the first time since he'd found her with a gun to her head, Eli saw relief and strength returning to her gaze. "I remember. You know I don't like surprises."

"Shut up," Roderick said. "We've got to find that boy and get him off this plane."

"And what will happen to us when we do that?" Eli asked, scanning the plane as he talked. He saw a movement near the small front storage compartment. Scotty?

Roderick snickered. "Only the boy and I get off this

plane today, sir. The rest of you will have to fly away. That's the plan."

Eli knew better than that. They'd probably all end up dead if those thugs on the ground had their way.

He watched the storage compartment, figuring Scotty was right there, listening and waiting. Then he glanced back at Gena. "Get ready," he shouted just as he felt the plane shift and groan. "Scotty, hold on!"

Eli held to a seat, his eyes on the surprised Roderick. "If this plane takes off, you'll still be on it with us, Roderick. Think about that."

Brice was bringing the big plane into a fast spin. And before he could grab hold of anything else, Eli was propelled right toward Gena and Roderick, giving him enough momentum to knock the gun away from Gena's head. Eli heard the explosion as the gun went off, then watched as they both went backward toward the galley cabinets. Gena didn't waste any time. She turned and kneed Roderick in the stomach. He groaned as his hands went flying to his mid-section. The gun clattered to the floor and slid underneath a seat. Eli took over where Gena left off, sending a jarring blow to Roderick's already-bruised midsection. The steward went down and was out for the count while Eli retrieved the gun.

"Are you hit?" Eli asked Gena, his gaze searching her face.

"No," she said, winded but coherent. "Scotty?" Gena pushed away from Eli, then crawled up the aisle even as the big plane started a clumsy climb.

Eli thought he heard bullets hitting the plane, but maybe that was just his heart hitting against his chest.

"Gena?"

He followed her, holding tight to the seats as the plane's nose lifted into the early-morning sky. Then he looked up as Gena and Scotty rolled out of the storage closet and fell onto a nearby seat. Eli rushed to join them, holding on to Gena as they protected Scotty with their bodies.

He was still holding her when the plane finally leveled out. While it was good to be holding her close knowing that she and Scotty were both still alive, Eli let go and sprung into action. He was going to beat that traitor of a steward into a pulp.

"Eli, stop!"

Only Gena's voice inside his rage-filled head stopped Eli from hitting the skinny man lying on the floor.

"He's…he's not conscious," she said, her words breathless in Eli's ears, her hand covering his raised fist. "Don't do anything you'll regret."

Eli sank back in the aisle, heaving a great breath. "I should…I should. He has a lot to answer to."

"Is he alive?"

Eli checked Roderick's pulse. "Yes, he's alive. Between the two of us, we knocked him out cold, but we didn't kill him." Because Gena had stopped him from doing further harm, Eli tried to revive Roderick.

"Let's get him into a seat," Gena suggested. "Maybe I can get some water down him."

Touched by her compassion, considering the man had been holding a gun to her head just minutes earlier, Eli did as Gena asked. Then he examined Roderick again. "He's not shot. Probably cracked a few ribs, though."

Brice came charging up the aisle. "Is everything okay?"

"Who's flying the plane?" Scotty asked, sniffing back sobs.

"Mr. Vern knows how to handle the plane," Brice assured him. "Are you all right, Scotty?"

"Yes, sir. Mom?"

"I'm fine, honey. Just fine." Gena moved away from Roderick's still body to sit with Scotty. "Let's just stay in our seats."

Brice pulled Eli out of the way. "You showed remarkable restraint. I thought I'd find the man dead."

Eli glanced toward Gena. "I seriously considered that, but someone stopped me."

Brice lifted a dark brow. "Aye, I can see. It's amazing to behold."

"Just shut up and help me get him awake. I want to find out who sent him."

Brice nodded. "I've instructed Vern to take us to south Louisiana. New Orleans. Kissie can help."

Eli let out a groan. "I was hoping to avoid getting Kissie involved in this."

"She's a good woman, Eli. She's on your side."

"I trust Kissie more than most. I just don't want to put her in harm's way. And right now, I'm not sure who's on my side."

Gena shot out of her seat. "We're all on your side, whether you want us here or not. And I only ask that if someone offers you help, you accept, because I'd like to keep my son alive." Motioning to Roderick, she said, "Now get him up so we can question him."

Eli gave Brice a contrite look. "Smart woman."

"Too smart for the likes of you."

"Let's do this. We have to make him talk."

Brice leaned over Roderick, then tugged at his uniform. "Wake up, sleepyhead. We've got to go over some things with you." He looked back up at Eli. "I'm sorry, brother. Sorry I let him get so close."

Eli was sorry, too. Sorry he'd ever brought this on Gena and the boy. But also very thankful that he was here in the thick of things to protect them.

"I didn't want to do it, honestly."

Roderick gulped the water Gena brought him, then shook his head, his Adam's apple bobbing in his thin neck, his eyes bulging like cue balls as he clutched his bruised body.

"Let's just go over this one more time," Eli said, careful to keep his voice down. Brice was back in the cockpit and Gena was reading to Scotty to keep him calm. They had only about thirty minutes before landing near New Orleans and Eli planned to make the most of that time.

Roderick put down the glass of water, his hands shaking. "All I know is that someone approached me at my apartment in Atlanta. I told you, I live there and work for Mr. Whelan from his Atlanta base as needed. He has a house there."

"So you've said," Eli retorted, pinching his nose between his forefinger and thumb. "So these people who approached you knew certain things about you and your family?"

"Yes, sir. Too many things. They said I had to cooperate with them or…someone close to me might get hurt. They threatened my mom and dad. And they knew exactly where to find them, too."

Eli nodded, holding up a hand so the kid wouldn't start blabbering again. "I understand. Now tell me exactly what they wanted you to do, Roderick."

"They wanted me to spy on Mr. Whelan. Then they mentioned your name. I didn't know who you were, but they explained things to me real good and proper. Said you were a friend of Mr. Whelan and that I needed to let them know when you two made contact."

Eli's head shot up. "And how did you manage that?"

"I…I bugged one of Mr. Whelan's computers and one of his cell phones," Roderick said with a shrug. "I'm a senior at Georgia Tech, majoring in bioinformatics."

As if that explained everything, Eli thought. "Go on."

"I heard another man telling Mr. Whelan that you were in trouble and he needed to head to Maine. I got the location and then I reported back."

So that's how they'd kept tabs. Through some scared college student who worked part-time for Brice. "What else?" he said, his voice deadly calm now.

"I bided my time," Roderick said. "I figured he'd need the jet sooner or later. I was ready to go and I knew what I had to do."

"What kind of instructions did they give you?"

"They came to me again, in the middle of the night with guns on me, and told me that I had to act normal, but that I had to make sure I got the little boy off the plane the minute it landed. I had to give them our itinerary, too. I texted that to them the minute we took off."

"Of course you did." Eli waited as Brice's voice announced the landing. "Tell me, Roderick, can you give me a description of these people, any more information that might help us?" He leaned close, his hand pressing into Roderick's rail-thin arm. "It might help your case immensely."

"What are y'all gonna do with me?" Roderick asked, terror coloring his eyes. "And what about my parents? They're not in the best of health. I'm worried about them."

"We'll take care of your parents. I'll get someone to them right away, but first you have to help me."

Roderick let out a sigh of relief. "I remember seeing something that might help, I think."

"Tell me," Eli said, his tone leaving no doubt.

"When you were on the laptop, I...kinda did some spying then, too. They told me to be ever watchful. And I saw a company logo on one of the pages you were reading."

"What did it say? What kind of logo?"

"Prowler, I think. The logo was black and gold—like a panther's head. Some kind of security company maybe?"

Eli sent Gena a grim glance. Prowler was one of the companies Gena worked for—she kept their Web site up-to-date. He'd been checking out anyone she might have been involved with, hoping to find a hint. "I know what you're talking about. Why does that ring a bell?"

Roderick's eyes widened. "Because one of the men who threatened me was wearing a ring that had that same symbol on it—a black panther with two gold eyes. Two yellow diamonds for eyes from what I could tell. I remember it because he held a gun so close to my face, that ring was all I could see. When I saw that on the Web page, I nearly dropped your coffee cup. It reminded me of that night and how those men had threatened me. You can't imagine what a nervous wreck I've been these last few days. But I didn't have any choice."

Eli patted Roderick on his arm. "You've redeemed yourself, Roderick, and now you've made the right choice. We might be able to salvage you yet."

"And my parents?"

Eli held up his phone. "Just give me their address and I'll send a team to check on them."

Roderick rattled off an address in central Georgia. "I hope we're not too late. I failed at my mission. They said they'd kill them if I didn't deliver the boy."

Eli punched at the phone. "You let me worry about that.

And just be glad that your mission changed. You've saved that little boy's life. That should make your parents very proud."

When he glanced over at Gena, her eyes held a look of awe. Apparently he'd just made *her* proud, too. That shouldn't feel so good, but it did. For once, he'd used compassion instead of his fists. And because of that, the woman he was falling in love with had been proud of him.

And…his son was still alive.

For now.

FIFTEEN

"Here's the low-down."

Kissie swung around in her swivel chair, her chocolate-colored eyes scanning Eli's face. She had gospel music blasting on the computer just in case anyone was trying to listen in.

"I'm ready." He sat down next to her in the hidden room at her house in New Orleans.

The place located in the Quarter and known locally as Kissie's Korner was also a coffee shop with an eclectic mixture of live gospel and blues music on most nights. This was not only Kissie's cover while she worked behind the scenes as a CHAIM agent, but also served as a haven for teens in trouble. Kissie had saved many a lost soul, including Eli. Eli trusted her with his life, but he wasn't so sure he was ready to hear her report on Prowler Security.

Kissie handed him a thick folder. "Gena and I went over everything with a fine-toothed comb, but she only knew what she had to know to get her job done. This is a very secretive company for obvious reasons. The poor woman's exhausted and shocked, so I didn't push her for more information right now. I'm glad she finally went upstairs to rest."

"Me, too," Eli said, his hand tight on the folder. "Both she and the boy are tired."

"You look tired yourself," Kissie responded. "Want some more coffee?"

"*Non.* I just want to get on with this and get them out of here. Any word from Brice?"

"He landed in Atlanta. And Roderick's parents are all right. Brice is bringing them to Atlanta to be with their son until the authorities can figure out how to handle this situation. He also let Dev know that everyone is alive and well. Dev is not happy with you, by the way."

Eli ignored that. He'd deal with Devon later. He was glad to hear Brice had been able to save Roderick's parents. And he was glad for Brice's help—even now Brice was digging into the what and why of this situation. Eli owed his friend a second chance. And he thanked God for giving him a lot of second chances lately. He'd come out of a cold, dark, desolate place to find hope again. In his son and in God. He needed a lot of help to make that happen now.

"You decide where you're going next?" Kissie asked, bringing him out of his thoughts.

"Yes, and we leave tonight, if possible." He saw Kissie's disapproval in her pursed lips. "It's the only way, Kiss. I can't tell you where—too risky, and besides you'd just tell Devon and Brice. I have to do this on my own. I have to find some sort of link between this company and the Peacemaker."

"Might find all you need right here," Kissie said, her long cornrows falling into precision across her silk blouse as she indicated the file on the desk. "Go on, read it."

Eli read the first few pages, then threw it back on the

desk. "So it's just as Roderick said. Prowler Security Systems is a big deal. And from the looks of things, this company obviously has some very strong ties with CHAIM. Secret ties."

"One of our approved security companies," Kissie said. "Which is why Gena was doing business with them in the first place. Devon thought she'd be safe working for CHAIM-sanctioned companies. Prowler set up part of our own state-of-the-art security and encryption files so that means someone within CHAIM approved them."

"*Oui*, and based on this information, we both can figure who that someone was and that this company has most likely been spying on his behalf since the beginning." Eli got up to pace the few feet between them. "My grandfather can't let things alone, even dead. He must have kept tabs on all of us so he could always be one step ahead of us."

"So what now?"

Eli took the report. "I have to tell Gena. And then we're getting out of here. They might even have your files loaded with malware."

"I was careful," Kissie assured him. "Without going into technical detail, let's just say I worked my way around anything questionable by using another system and rerouting all inquiries in untraceable code. I didn't even go through the regular CHAIM system. I'm thinking this can't be good, no good at all."

"You and me both." He gave her a quick hug, then turned to leave. "I'm going to wake Gena."

But he wasn't sure how he was going to explain all of this to her. Gena would not like hearing that she'd been working for the man who was trying to take their son.

* * *

Gena heard a knock at the door and immediately sat straight up in bed, her heart pulsing a warning throughout her groggy system. "Who is it?"

"Eli."

Running a hand through her hair, she pulled her sweater around her and rushed to the door. She'd had a long shower and a change of clothes earlier, but suddenly she was so cold again. When she opened the door, she was shivering, maybe from fear and maybe from a glaring aftershock to all that had happened so far.

Eli took one look at her and pulled her into his arms. "Are you all right?"

"Cold," she said. "So cold."

"It's much warmer here than in Maine, at least," he told her, his big hand stroking her hair. "I can find you another robe or sweater or turn up the heat."

"No," she said, pulling him toward her. She suddenly needed his nearness. She hated to admit weakness, but he was so warm and solid and she needed that right now. She realized she hadn't felt safe in a very long time, long before these horrible people had tried to take Scotty. But with Eli, she felt a warmth and a security that had long been missing in her life. And she thanked God for allowing her this brief bit of contentment even if it did confuse her to no end.

Eli pulled her close, kissing her hair as he whispered something soothing and sweet in French to her. Gena didn't care that she couldn't understand it. She just knew that the words were endearing and beautiful.

Finally, she lifted her head and looked up at him, afraid he'd see what was in her heart. "I'm better now."

Eli stared down at her with a sweet longing that echoed inside her soul. "Are you sure?"

She nodded. "I was just startled when you knocked. I need to go check on Scotty."

Eli held her tight, then whispered in her ear. "He's fine. He's asleep. Kissie has a guard on him. He's right across the hall in my room and the door is open. The guard is facing the windows to make sure no one has access. And Kissie has a very good alarm system with hidden cameras."

Gena wanted to trust that, but lately trust had become a precious commodity. Eli led her to a sofa near the door, his voice still low. "Sit here where we can see. I'll leave the door open, so we can keep an eye on the guard and Scotty."

She sank down on the high-backed Victorian sofa, her gaze on the dark door across the hallway where a man sat in a chair just a few feet from Scotty's bed. "What did you find out?"

He thumped the file he'd been holding, once again cautioning her with a finger to his lips to speak quietly. "Kissie managed to dig a little deeper after you came upstairs."

"Okay." She knew that Prowler Security belonged to a man named Kenneth Crane and that she worked for that man as part of his Web site team. He had teams all over the country and Gena worked for several other clients. "Mr. Crane is a powerful man, but I don't understand how he could be involved in any of this. He's a humanitarian and philanthropist and his company is one of the best."

"*Oui,* but what better way to spy on you and my child than with his own equipment and what better way to get inside CHAIM—we approved him and gave him our blessings—than to set himself up as do-gooder and all-around nice guy? Someone high up in CHAIM certainly thought that—or didn't care either way."

"Your grandfather?" She didn't have to see his frown to know it was the truth. "Oh, Eli."

"From what we can gather, my grandfather and Mr. Crane were old friends. They traveled in the same high-class circles in both Texas and Louisiana. Old money, oil and gas and technology. My grandfather handpicked Crane to install elaborate systems on most of CHAIM's computers and inside several of our headquarters and offices. Kissie had to do most of our digging through other resources just to find out this much."

Gena bobbed her head. "Prowler is the best at advanced technology—their data encryption programs are the industry standard. They're developing a system for what we call vaporizing data."

Eli frowned. "Does that mean what I think it means?"

"It means they can make computer files disappear. Even on a hard drive. That's probably one of the main reasons CHAIM was so intrigued with this company, that and their biometric tracking systems. I wish I knew more, but then I tried to never ask questions. I just built sites based on their specifications. And signed an oath of silence about what little I learned."

"While they spied on you at will. And apparently erased anything they wanted to from our system."

"Apparently. But why, Eli? I mean, even if Mr. Crane knows Scotty is your son, why would he come after you like this? Why would he want to harm Scotty and what would he have to gain by destroying you?"

"Maybe because we stopped his gravy train—his inside connections with CHAIM—when the Peacemaker died. Or maybe…because he was afraid he'd be exposed for doing something illegal without my grandfather as his shield. That's the part I can't figure."

Gena got up to stare out into the muted light from the hallway, watching as the guard looked around the door and nodded at her. Coming back, she whispered, "Do you realize the magnitude of this, Eli? This is a global company headed by an apparently ruthless man. As I said, I don't know much about him, but I do know that Prowler Security works with everyone from the Navy to major hotels to private companies on helping to protect their technology. They deal in cryptographic snapshots and behavioral biometrics."

"Okay, explain that word *biometrics* to me. It's in Kissie's report, but I didn't take the time to read all the details."

"You use it every time you touch your phone or log on to a CHAIM laptop. It's a highly sensitive physiological identification system, based on fingerprints, iris scans, even vocal cords. It's a big deal for security purposes because it's used for employee identification. This type of system virtually assures that a corporation or organization won't allow anyone who isn't within the biometrics database to get through. And it only takes about a second for the scan to recognize someone with a biometric ID."

Eli put down the file, then stood to face her. "So what if Crane has been illegally tracking people by using biometrics as some sort of spyware and he's afraid someone will stumble on that?"

Gena couldn't answer that. "Kissie can probably tell you more because she's the real computer whiz, but I'd guess CHAIM uses equipment from Prowler to keep track of all its agents and to verify identities. But someone who knew what he was doing could take this technology and set up a biometric template that might read false—to get into a system or organization illegally. Or to pretend to be someone else."

"Crane and my grandfather would both qualify for doing something like that. And if Crane had been forced to do this per the Peacemaker, then he'd certainly hold a grudge."

"But why would he come after Scotty? I don't know anything about that and you sure don't, so why pick on us?"

"Maybe my grandfather *did* force Crane to do something illegal," Eli said, his expression grim. "And if I know my grandfather, he was probably holding that over Crane's head. It would make sense that my grandfather needed someone to implant an undetectable spyware system within CHAIM's elaborate computer system. He must have found out something about Crane and then handpicked his company for that very reason."

"And Crane's afraid you have that information now, so he decides to kidnap your son to blackmail you? Or to get to the information before someone else does?"

"Yes, and easy for him to find me and you, because he knows exactly how to trace us. The only thing I don't understand is how my grandfather found out about you and Scotty in the first place."

Gena let out a gasp. "Probably by accident. Think about it. All that happened to you would have been reported on the CHAIM network. If your grandfather was as conniving as you say, he would have immediately put out feelers about you and about—"

"My missing pregnant wife—the one he thought he'd killed," Eli finished. "He probably knew exactly what Devon was up to, trying to save Leah and my baby. But instead of stepping into things, he just bided his time out of fear of being caught red-handed with all his illegal deeds—until I came home. Who knows what might have happened to Scotty if the Peacemaker had killed both Devon and me."

Gena hated the look of disgust and agony on his face. She didn't want to think about such an evil man controlling her son. "Eli, I'm so sorry."

His expression was as grim and dark as the Mississippi River. "Don't be, *chère*. I gave up on being sorry about the Peacemaker a long time ago."

Gena wanted to tell him that one day he was going to have to let go of his bitterness and forgive his grandfather, but right now she couldn't bring herself to suggest that. Right now, she only wanted her son safe and she'd do whatever needed to be done to make that happen.

Eli was silent for a minute, his dark eyes bright with realization and regret. "It's a stretch but we might be onto something, and this would certainly explain why my grandfather left everything to me. He would hope I'd get caught holding the cookie jar, and with all this technology he could easily set things up to make me look like the culprit. I just have to find out exactly what kind of surprise he's left for me and somehow, I have to convince Crane we don't have anything on him."

"Except now we do," she whispered.

"But he doesn't know that yet."

Gena couldn't imagine anyone being so cunning and evil. This was the worst form of abuse—to torment someone with such calculation and cruelty. "How do we prove it?"

Eli touched a hand to her chin, admiring her bravery and her determination. He'd never before known a woman like

Gena. She was as fierce and brave as any CHAIM agent, but then, she had a mother's love to give her strength. Sending up a silent prayer for God to help him do the right thing by this woman and their child, he said, "First, we get out of here. We have to try to find some kind of evidence so that we can stop Crane from coming after Scotty."

Gena's eyes widened while she let the implication of his words soak in. Finally, she took a deep, steadying breath. "Okay. I'll get ready."

Eli nodded, then turned for the door. "I'll get us some provisions and come back for you." He pivoted around, needing to make her see how she made him feel. "Gena—"

"Don't tell me you're sorry, Eli. If you hadn't come to find us, I don't know what might have happened. We're in this together now."

That was all the encouragement he needed to pull her back into his arms. "*Oui,* together. I like the sound of that." He touched a finger to her trailing hair. "I've been apart from everyone and everything I've loved. I've been alone. But since I've found you and Scotty, I...I've found hope again. I need you both to be in my life. Together, Gena, all three of us." Then he lowered his head to kiss her, hoping his touch would convey what was inside his heart. He was afraid to let go of this shield of torment, afraid he'd become worse off than he'd ever been before because he was so terrified of losing this fragile connection to hope. But with Gena, and with his son, it would be worth that risk.

When he ended the kiss, he looked down at her to make sure he hadn't misread things. The awareness in her eyes told him what he needed to know. She felt the same. But he wanted to hear her say it. "What's happening between us, *chère?*"

She touched a hand to his shirt collar. "I'm not sure but…it's growing on me. *You're* growing on me. I never expected this to happen, so I'm a little shaky right now." Then she backed away. "I'll need some time…after this is over."

"You mean to see if this thing between us is real?"

"Yes."

She didn't have to explain things to Eli. He understood the intensity of their time together. When things settled down and his one prayer was to see that happen, then they could slow down and really get to know each other. And he could at last enjoy being with his son.

He tugged her back. "When this is over, *catin,* I promise I will show you exactly what's real between us. We will become boring and normal and we will figure this out in a secluded place where we can take our time and become a family, you, me and Scotty."

"You, normal?" She smiled, her beauty wrapping around Eli's heart like a soft satin ribbon. "I highly doubt that."

"Well, as close to normal as a ragin' Cajun can be."

She grinned, then turned serious again. "Where are you taking us, Eli?"

He touched a finger to her nose. "To the ends of the earth. We're going to Grand Isle, Louisiana. And once we're there, I intend to find the truth."

SIXTEEN

"**Y**ou really did bring us to the ends of the earth."

Gena looked out the van window, seeing water on each side of the long bridge snaking over Caminada Bay. In the early-morning sunrise the two-lane strip of winding road seemed to disappear right into the salt marshes and tidal ponds, making it seem as if they and the old van, too, were disappearing straight into the water. When the bridge lifted and curved to the island, in spite of her fatigue and worries, she let out a gasp of pleasure.

"Eli, it's beautiful."

"*Oui.*" Eli glanced over at her. "I grew up on the island. The only blemish on this eight-mile stretch of land is the house my grandfather owned and left to me. He called it a camp house because he used it as a fishing retreat. But it's a bit more than that, I think. It's where my parents fell in love one summer. I've never liked his home." He shrugged, as if that explained everything.

Gena gave him a silent look, knowing he'd tell her everything in his own good time. He'd been very quiet since they'd left New Orleans. The man talked a lot about his grandfather, but never his father and he said very little about his mother. Gena knew his pain on that subject ran so deep, she wouldn't dare question him. But now, she needed answers on what he hoped to gain by bringing them to Grand Isle. "But you're taking us to his house. Why?"

His eyes shimmered with the same unfathomable depths of the swirling water around them. "Because if I know my grandfather, he left something inside that house to either hinder me or help me. He knew I loved this island, so he probably assumed I'd come back here one day. He knew exactly where to find me after my father died. And he knew exactly how to get to me. He's trying to do that still. Only now it's my turn. Kenneth Crane shouldn't be able to trace us here since few people know that my grandfather owned this place. That gives me time to find the truth and make sure Mr. Crane pays for his crimes, same as my grandfather."

Gena hated the vindictive tone in his voice. "Eli, remember we're in this together. Don't do anything to jeopardize things. If you do, you might lose Scotty forever."

He gave her a harsh stare. "You're not threatening me, now, are you, *chère?*"

"No. *I'm* not the threat here. I'm on your side. Your biggest threat right now is yourself. If you go into this set on revenge, it won't work and it won't help Scotty. Please, do this the right way, for me and for your own sake?"

He watched the road for a minute, then glanced back over at her. "Still think I'm a lost cause?"

Gena turned toward the back seat to make sure Scotty was asleep, then she reached for Eli's hand. "No, I think you're a cause worth fighting for and I hope that makes a difference with you."

He didn't respond. He just drove along the winding highway, but in a few minutes, he eased the rickety van

Kissie had secured for them off the road. Near a flat stretch of marshland, a broken, weathered house missing part of its roof stood like a dark sentinel at the mouth of the island. Water lapped greedily at the thick moorings underneath the crooked house, while graceful white egrets moved like ballerinas in the tall grasses near the steps. Turning off the motor, he sat staring at the run-down house, his expression etched in the dueling shadows and lights of the reluctant dawn. "You see that place? That's where I grew up, right there in that little shack. The first thing I saw out my bedroom windows every morning when I woke up was water—salt marshes on one side and the Gulf of Mexico on the other.

"The recent hurricanes pretty much destroyed everything on this island in one way or another and shifted the landscape. That house is in water now because the ocean is taking away bits and pieces of this land, inch by inch." He stopped, inhaled, then hit his hand on the steering wheel. "And that's exactly how I've felt most of my life. CHAIM and my grandfather did that to me—took away bits and pieces of me, Gena, inch by inch, all in the name of God. When I realized down in South America that my own grandfather might be corrupt and that he'd tried to draw me into that corruption, I got physically ill. I had set too much store in that man, had hoped to make him proud, make him love me. He never allowed my father to love my mother and me, so I prayed he was trying to make amends. But I was wrong, so wrong.

"Then when things went bad and they took Leah, I wanted to die. I turned from God, Gena. I turned from God because I blamed Him for taking the woman I loved, for taking my unborn child, for taking the very things that made me breathe. I didn't want to live and I thought He had abandoned me just like my father had to abandon us. But I think maybe it was the other way around. I think I had never actually accepted God into my life, even though I'd taken an oath with CHAIM to serve Him. I didn't want to serve anyone anymore. I only wanted whoever had done this to feel the same kind of pain I'd felt."

He wiped his eyes, gritted his teeth, looked at the dilapidated old shack. "I'm so tired, so very tired. I was hoping this time things might be different. But I'm still fighting against some force—something or someone. I'm tired of fighting and I'm wondering if I can survive this fight and save Scotty. I'm wondering if maybe you both *would* have been better off without me in your life."

Gena's tears left a salty trail down her face and her heart felt as if someone had pierced it with a fishing hook, but she held on to Eli's arm, her gaze entreating him to listen to her. "But you made it through, Eli. You made it through because you found something to live for again. You have something to fight for, something *worth* the fight. Don't give up on that now."

He groaned, inhaling another racking breath. His voice went so low that she had to strain to hear him. "*Oui,* I did. I found…my son. And right now, that is the only thing holding me together. You and the boy, Gena. You and the boy—I have to keep that image front and center or—"

"Or you'll go back to that other place? That's what you're afraid of, I know, but we're here. And we need you to stay here with us. Please, Eli, please? Don't give up now. You can't."

She moved toward him, her hands on his face, her kisses

tasting his tears. Then she closed her eyes and said a prayer. "Please, Christ, be with us. Be with us."

Eli let out a shattered sob, then pulled her into his arms, his dark eyes watching her. "I can't go through that again, understand? I can't."

"You won't have to," she said, wondering how she could make such a claim. "I won't let you."

She kissed him there by the water, by the ramshackle, desolate house, with the sun coming up over the horizon in golden-washed hues of pink and mauve like an awakening. Gena held him, her whispered prayers rising up through the sunrays with each breath she took, with each kiss she placed on his scarred skin. "We can do this. We have to do this," she said. "Eli?"

He finally looked into her eyes, his torment so raw she almost turned away. But she kept her eyes on him to reassure him even though his next words didn't hold out much hope. "You can't make that promise, *belle*. You can't and we both know it."

"But *He* can," Gena said, her words firm with resolve. "He can, Eli. Trust in that. Trust that He hasn't brought you through all that pain just to make you suffer again. There has to be a reason for this—for your finding us."

"How can I trust?" he asked, his hands pulling through her hair. "How can I trust, Gena? Show me."

Gena put a hand to his heart. "You have to let go of all that pain and fear. You're one of the bravest men I've ever known, except for when it comes to going on faith. You have to do the right thing and trust that God will see you through all the darkness. And you have to trust that no matter what happens, good or bad, God will be there with you throughout, Eli. You have to believe that.

You've been through so much, but look where it's brought you. Look what you've found." She glanced over the seat at her sleeping little boy. "Scotty loves you. I know he does. And you've shown me how much you love him."

Eli pulled her back into his arms and held her. He didn't speak again, but Gena watched as his lips moved in a whispered prayer. Watched and accepted that she was in love with this man and that she would help him to end this so that he could find his soul again. And in the process, she could find her own strength. For the sake of their child.

He drove off the main road onto a secluded, narrow lane encroached with ancient live oaks dripping with Spanish moss. They came upon a graveyard, its mausoleums and tombstones shimmering white and silvery gray in the rising dawn. The graves were surrounded by Confederate jasmine about to bud yellow blossoms and thick oleander and hibiscus bushes that had yet to bloom. The old road cut like a ribbon right through the middle of the cemetery.

Gena stared out the window at a stone cherub watching over a small grave—a child's grave. Faded plastic pastel flowers, toppled and leaning, sat here and there amid the grave markers and the stone-encased enclosures. It was so quiet that not even a bird chirped. Even the wind seemed unsure about entering this place.

"Where are we?" she asked, glancing ahead as the van bounced through an open rusty wrought-iron gate with two fleurs-de-lis centered on each side of its slender bars.

When Eli didn't answer her, she looked up through the mossy trees toward a weathered two-story white house that sat facing the cemetery on one side and the ocean on the other. Already, she could hear the crashing waves just past the sand dunes and sea oats surrounding the long, flat yard. When she looked past Eli, she saw the bay shimmering to the right beyond the overgrown cemetery. They were almost completely surrounded by water, but she reminded herself this was a small island and they weren't that far from the main highway, the only road out.

"Is this the house?"

Eli nodded, stopping near a dark, gnarled tree that held cobalt-blue glass bottles, some extended on old worn ropes along its branches, others just stuck on the ends of slender, jagged limbs. Gena stared at the tree, thinking it was almost beautiful the way the bottles rattled as they hit against the branches and each other while the timid wind blew across the island.

Eli saw her looking at the tree. "Voodoo," he said. "The bottles are to ward off evil spirits. Pierre Savoy pretended to believe in God, but he delved in all kinds of spiritual quests, especially in South America. And I'm sure he had many reasons to worry about evil spirits."

"Then why did he have a house by a cemetery?"

Eli shrugged. "The house was here first. It's been in the Savoy family for generations. Most of the people buried in the cemetery are my ancestors—some of the less fortunate ones, at least. He has another house in New Orleans, a mighty nice Garden District mansion where he watched Lydia almost die from a reaction to pesticides that he had provided and paid someone to put in her body lotion. He tended to force underlings with weaknesses to do his dirty work."

Gena closed her eyes as a shudder went through her body. "Do we have to stay here?"

"Only long enough for me to search the place."

She turned to check on Scotty. The little boy was sitting up, rubbing his eyes. "Where are we, Mom?"

Eli gave Gena a warning look, then turned to Scotty. "We're on Grand Isle, where I grew up."

Scotty squinted toward the brilliant water all around them, then pointed. "Is that a big lake?"

"That?" Eli said, grinning for the first time since they'd left Maine, "Well, now, *that's* the Gulf of Mexico. And this is *my* ocean."

He heard laughter out on the beach.

Eli looked up from the old secretary desk in his grandfather's small study inside the Creole-style house.

Taking a few precious seconds to walk over to the open French doors leading out onto the long gallery, he watched as Gena and Scotty walked along the rich gray-colored sand. Eli leaned against the peeling white paint of the door frame, the sight of his son running in front of Gena causing his breath to catch. Gena's long, dark hair lifted out in the brisk winds off the Gulf, while Scotty's equally dark curls danced and shimmered against his forehead. The carefree picture presented a facade that tore at Eli's heart.

He loved them both.

He had to save them.

So he turned back to his work. Tedious, this, because the Peacemaker had left none of the gadgets and fancy equipment and tools of their trade here. No smart phones, no laptops, no surveillance equipment or listening devices, no flash drives or computer discs of any kind.

No hint of what kind of trap he'd set for Eli this time.

Frustrated, Eli started his search again, lifting papers, shuffling through files, trying to find a clue, anything else that might connect Kenneth Crane to Pierre Savoy. He sat down at the desk, retracing everything that had happened in the last few years, beginning with the fiasco down in South America.

"Think, Eli," he told himself. They'd gone down there to rescue a teenaged girl who'd run away to join a cult deep in the jungles of Rio Branco. Their superiors had sent in Devon and Eli with a few junior recruits for backup. "It should have been easy," Eli thought now, remembering how worried he'd been about leaving Leah so late in her pregnancy. He'd promised her he'd be home in time for the baby's arrival, but they got so bogged down in trying to locate the cult and the girl that things had dragged out.

And then, impatient and ready to be done with it, Eli had gone off on his own and stumbled upon something he'd never forget. He'd found evidence that Pierre Savoy, known in CHAIM circles as the Peacemaker, could possibly have a major connection to the drugs being shipped in and out of South America. Little did he know that his own grandfather was also a powerful cult leader. Eli had found that out too late. Too late for the girl and too late for his family.

The girl had been killed when the cult had sent henchmen to stop CHAIM. And from what Eli had learned over the years following that mission, her parents had never forgiven CHAIM for failing to rescue her.

"What was her name?" he said, trying to remember. "Katie, Kali?" Kali. Dark-haired and skinny, scared and a drug addict. He didn't know her last name. But he remembered her face. She had resisted them from the get-go because she didn't want to go back home.

To Texas.

She'd made a comment in all her ranting about hating Texas. Kenneth Crane lived in Texas.

Eli started searching all around the desk again, his heart pumping as he tried to recall some of the things the girl had said to them. He'd been too busy trying to save her life to listen to her angry profanity and protests.

"His wrath will come down on you!"

Eli could see her face contorted in pain and rage. Had Kali been talking about the Peacemaker or someone else?

But no, her parents had wanted her home. But who were her parents? Eli had never learned their identity because CHAIM was very careful with confidentiality in situations such as this. One whispered name in the wrong place could bring harm to innocent people. So they'd only had the girl's first name to go on. And not much else except an order to get her away from the cult.

Which we failed to do, he thought as he kept searching. Then his hand hit on a tiny compartment in one of the many cubbyholes of the old desk. Eli pushed at the little door and felt it click open to a long flat hiding place.

He pulled out a rumpled envelope and quickly opened it to reveal a stack of aged papers and photos. Hurrying through the papers, he found two pictures. And knew he'd just discovered what he needed.

One of the pictures was of him and Kali. They were on a boat and he was talking to her. Okay, so that proved *he'd* been with the girl in Rio Branco. But that just meant his grandfather had been watching him. Another picture showed his grandfather laughing with Kenneth Crane. It looked as if they'd been on a fishing trip. Eli turned it over and saw some numbers and letters written in permanent ink. Followed by the words "Now that which decayeth and waxeth old is ready to vanish away."

From *Hebrews*. What did it mean? Did his grandfather write this? Something clicked in Eli's mind as he thought back over all the information they'd gathered on Crane.

Not vanished, but *vaporized*. Gena had said Crane's technology could make computer files go away. Vanish? But what if not all of the incriminating files were gone?

"He's after us because of this?"

Eli went back through the papers until he stumbled upon some sort of contract. And that's when his heart stopped.

It was a copy of the contract someone had signed with CHAIM. The work order that stated Kenneth Crane was hiring CHAIM to go down to Brazil and get Kali Crane. The contract stated that CHAIM had his permission to bring his daughter back to Texas.

His daughter.

Eli dropped the contract and stared at the picture.

The girl who had died that day in the jungle was the daughter of Kenneth Crane. And Pierre Savoy's signature was on the contract. Eli understood the implications, but why had his grandfather left this here?

Grabbing the contract, Eli read back over it. As he turned to the second page, a note fluttered out:

"His wrath will come down on you."

Shocked, he remembered that's exactly what Kali had said the day they'd tried to rescue her.

Had the girl been trying to warn them?

And had his grandfather left this to warn him, too? And to give him the proof he needed to save his son?

It was almost too much to believe. But then, the Peace-maker had been very good at riddles and puzzles and CHAIM lived by clues and codes.

Eli's cell rang, causing him to start. He opened it to find Kissie's code number listed. "What?"

"Eli, you have to hear this."

Eli went into high alert. Getting up, he looked outside. Gena and Scotty were sitting in an old swing near the shore. The sky was growing dark and he heard thunder off in the distance. "I think I know why."

"You found something?"

"Oui!" He explained the contract and the picture, then read her the passages. "What's going on there?"

Kissie confirmed what he'd found. "I traced things all the way back for about six years and pretty much discovered the same—the girl was Kenneth Crane's." She stopped. "Hold on, I alerted Brice earlier and he's sending me a code message from *Job* 36. 'Because there is wrath, beware lest He takes you away with one blow; For a large ransom would not help you to avoid it.'" She took a long breath. "I have more, Eli."

There was that word *wrath* again.

Eli hit the porch, then shouted to Gena. "Come inside." He pointed to the sky, but the coming rain was the least of his worries. Then he said into the phone, "Tell me something I don't know. This man wants an eye for an eye. He wants my son because he blames me for his daughter's death."

"Not you so much, Disciple. He blames your grandfa-ther. The Peacemaker kidnapped the girl and took her down there. He held her hostage because Crane had gotten tired of doing his bidding. Crane wanted out of all the spying, but your grandfather didn't like that. He took the girl and he got her hooked on drugs, hoping to convince Crane to stay quiet."

"And purposely killed her so she wouldn't talk," Eli finished. "That explains almost everything." And he thought he could put together the rest. His grandfather still had something on Crane and now Crane was gunning for Eli, hoping to find it.

Gena came up on the porch, her hand tight in Scotty's, her eyes questioning.

"I've got to go," Eli said, shutting his phone. He still didn't know if his grandfather had set a trap for him or if Kenneth Crane just wanted to make him suffer. Either way, it looked like Kali's father thought Eli was also to blame for all the man's troubles.

Either way, he had to get Gena and Scotty away from this house right now. Because he had a feeling that Mr. Crane would be arriving on this island very soon.

SEVENTEEN

"What's going on?"

Gena watched as Eli marched around the house, squinting out at the ocean and the bay. "Eli, what did you find out?"

"Enough," he said, shutting doors and pulling curtains together. "We need to leave."

"They know we're here?"

"Not sure. But there's a very good chance."

"But you said—"

He whirled to grab her by the arms. "I know what I said, but your guess is as good as mine right now."

Gena froze, turning cold and then flushing hot. "Tell me what you found."

"Not now. Too complicated." He went to where Scotty sat coloring on some paper Gena had gathered. "How would you like to take a boat ride around the island?"

Scotty hopped up. "Can we?"

"I don't see why not."

Eli motioned to Gena, then sat Scotty back in his chair at the long pine table in the kitchen. "Just finish your picture while I talk to your *maman,* okay?"

Scotty bobbed his head, then went back to his coloring. Gena waited for Eli to talk, her skin crawling with shivers of apprehension. If he was willing to take them out on a boat in what looked like a coming storm, things couldn't be in their favor. "It's bad, isn't it?"

"The worst." He told her about Kissie's call and what he'd found in the desk. "The girl who died down there— she was Crane's only daughter—Kali Crane. He's truly out for revenge."

"But it wasn't your fault."

"He's blaming me anyway and since the old man is dead, I reckon I'm next in line."

"But why did he wait until now?"

Eli motioned toward Scotty. "It took him this long to figure out that I had a son—he found my weakness, my blind spot. He probably heard it through the CHAIM channels right after things went down in Colorado with Devon and Lydia and me. As long as my grandfather was alive, Crane couldn't make a move without revealing his part in all of this. But now, well, it's open season. He probably thinks I've got the goods on him and I'll cave if he threatens my family. But the man has underestimated me—I won't cave and I won't let him come near either of you."

Gena shivered again. "What now?"

"We're leaving," Eli said. "But we can't take the road back out. There's a boat dock down on the bay side with a nice speedboat dry-docked there. I'm going down there to check it out." His expression said it all. "I need you to grab your jackets and have them ready, then stay right here and watch the boy. Lock the doors and don't leave this house. I'll be right back."

Gena didn't like that. "I'll watch out for you, too. If you're not back soon, we're coming to look for you."

"Give me fifteen minutes. Do not let anyone else in, you hear?"

"Okay." A spear of lightning brightened the sky out over the water, then thunder boomed like a cannon. "What about the storm?"

"We'll have to beat it. If I can get us to the other side of the island where it's more populated, we can hide out there for a while."

Eli checked the boat, cranking it to make sure it would still run. It had fuel and it seemed to be in good shape thanks to the enclosed boathouse where it had been raised out of the water by a small motorized pulley. If he could take it around the bay away from the crashing waves of the ocean, they might have a chance. The storm was rolling in with an all-out intensity and he'd have to hurry to get them safely around the pass to the other side of the island.

After he'd secured the boat by the floating dock, he turned to hurry back to the house, his gaze moving over the water and shore. So far, so good. He didn't see any approaching boats and the road and woods looked deserted, too. That didn't mean all was clear. His gut told him to get out of here.

"Should have never come here," he mumbled as he hurried to the house. But then, if he hadn't, he wouldn't have found the proof he needed to connect his grandfather to Crane. If Crane knew he had that contract and the picture, he'd come after Eli for sure. The man had grown desperate, worrying about what the Peacemaker had left behind. His plan had probably been to take Scotty in order to get Eli's cooperation on turning over any discriminating evidence. An eye for an eye. A child for a child.

Eli had enough of this type of justice. He didn't want to be a vigilante, but he'd do anything to protect Gena and Scotty. He'd tried to follow the rules, but now it was each man for himself. He had to put his family first.

He rushed through the trees, headed back toward the house. He made it to the crushed seashell lane leading from the dock to the yard when a man stepped out in front of him. A man holding a gun. And it was aimed right at Eli's head.

"This is courtesy of Mr. Crane. He said to tell you, you will never see your son again."

Eli acted purely on training and instinct, lifting up and around with a swift vertical kick to the man's throat. The attacker deflected it, then stumbled toward Eli. They went down together, scrabbling for the gun. The other man clutched the weapon, lifting it up as Eli flipped over. Then using the gun like a hammer on Eli's skull, he hit hard. Eli's world went dark.

Eli woke up to a pounding headache, rain washing over him as he lay in the dirt and mud on the old driveway. With a grunt, he came to, remembering what had happened. Adrenaline broke him awake and gasping. He stood, dizzy and disoriented, and pushed toward the house.

But he knew, he knew even with the rain rushing over him and the thunder and lightning blasting through the late afternoon, that he was too late. Again.

The wind picked up as he approached the house, causing the colored bottles to rattle like bones against the swaying bottle tree. The sky went velvet dark as lightning made a jagged dance out across the water. Huge, fat raindrops assaulted him, their sting welcoming. He hit the porch, taking the steps two at a time.

"Gena?"

She didn't answer.

"Gena? Scotty?"

Eli's heart slashed a path to match the lightning. He called again, his voice echoing throughout the rumble of thunder while pain pierced his skull. He moved through the dark house, his eyes scanning each room, his mind screaming with scenarios he didn't want to see. Grabbing a walking stick he saw in an old umbrella stand, he moved through the long central hallway.

"Gena?"

The house was empty.

Then he heard a noise outside. Footsteps hitting the porch. Eli whirled and headed toward the front of the house. And saw Gena and Scotty being pushed through the yard toward a waiting boat out on the water. While he'd been down at the docks, someone had managed to troll a small motorboat up to the Gulf-side shore. Which meant they'd been watching the house, waiting for just the right time to make a move.

Familiar reprimands echoed over and over inside his head, making him remember sickening things. *Why did I leave them alone? Why did I leave?* He rushed down to the beach, watching as the two men shoved Gena and Scotty along on the dark, wet sand. The rain hit fast and hard, blurring Eli's vision as he tried to belly crawl through the ground cover and the sea oats. He still had the walking stick but little else to use as a weapon. They were taking Gena and Scotty onto that tiny boat. It wouldn't survive the swift currents of the pass where the surging water merged in a deep, dangerous drop-off. He could rush them, but that might cause either one of them to get shot. And if he got shot, he wouldn't be able to help them.

Measuring the distance from the boathouse to the curve around the island into the ocean, Eli decided he'd have to make a run for the boat and get to them before they took off into the Gulf. It was his only hope.

Taking one last look at Gena and Scotty, he sent up a prayer, asking God to give him the courage to do this. Then he hopped up and ran as fast as he could for the boathouse.

Gena's prayers sat trapped inside a silent scream. She wanted to look back, sure she'd find Eli coming to help them. But these men had warned her the minute they'd pried open the lock and tiptoed into the house that if she spoke or tried to cry out, they'd shoot first and ask questions later.

These two weren't as sloppy as the others they'd had to deal with so far. They'd waited for the distraction of the storm to get into the house. They were hired assassins with big fancy guns and one of them was wearing a Prowler ring. She'd seen the panther's diamond eyes flashing at her as the man dragged her out the side door. They'd made it clear they were being paid to take the boy alive. But they didn't mind killing Gena. And she didn't want to think about what they'd done to Eli.

She had to stay quiet in order to stay with Scotty. It was the only way. She held his hand and willed him to be brave. He kept glancing up at her, his dark eyes so trusting, so hopeful but so terrified. He had to be thinking the same thing she was.

Where was Eli?

Eli waited for a round of thunder, then hit the switch to start the boat. It would be hard for anyone to hear in this wind, which was probably how these men had managed to get to the house in the first place. He'd use that same tactic to his advantage now. He slowly maneuvered the speedboat out from the floating dock, then carefully turned it toward the curve of the land toward the Gulf. With this wind and rain and the crashing, choppy sea, it wouldn't be easy to get to the other boat. But he had no other choice. It was now or never.

With one last prayer, he put the boat into full throttle and took off against the brutal wind and rain. He rounded the jutting curve into the white-capped waters of the Gulf of Mexico.

The other boat was already out in the open water just beyond the whitecaps, headed away from Eli. Hitting his hand on the control panel, Eli let out a fierce scream. And watched as Scotty's dark head disappeared in the rain and wind.

They were at some sort of marina. Gena looked around, wiping rain away from her eyes as she tried to memorize her surroundings. Shrimp boats were pulled up alongside million-dollar yachts and small watercrafts. Along the shore, houses of varying shapes and status sat right on the water. Why would they bring them to such a public place?

But then, the marina was deserted because of the storm and the approaching night. And to anyone watching, they were just a boat coming in out of the rain. Clutching Scotty close, she whispered, "Stay near me, honey."

He moved his head just an inch, but his hand was tight against hers. "Will he come for us, Mommy?"

Gena was glad the rain hid the tears forming inside her

eyes. "Yes, honey, he will." That she knew without a doubt. If Eli was still alive, he'd find them.

"Get out," one of the men said, yanking her by the arm.

Gena glared at him, but did as he told her. Both men were dressed in black rain slickers and they wore black baseball caps slung low over their eyes. It was hard to see either of them. And right now, Gena didn't care about identifying them. She had to figure out a way to get Scotty away from them.

One man stayed with the boat and headed back out into the bay while the other one guided them to a waiting black sedan. "Get in."

Gena's heart lurched in protest. If she got in that car, she probably wouldn't live to see the light of day. But she couldn't let Scotty go without her. "Where are we going?" she asked.

"Don't worry about that," her guard said. "Just get into the car and stay quiet." He leaned close. "Or I'll leave you here and take the boy."

Glancing around, she prayed someone would notice them. Her gaze caught a white-haired man sitting underneath a boat shelter, waiting for the storm to pass. Gena lifted her head toward him, just a quick motion. The man watched them, but he didn't move toward the car.

"I said get in."

Gena didn't take her eyes off the lone stranger sitting a few feet away. Pulling Scotty closer, she slid inside the dark car. What could she do to save her son? They were probably going to meet Kenneth Crane face-to-face at last. Gena would use the only weapon she had left. She'd use a mother's love to convince a grieving father that he couldn't do this.

* * *

Eli searched the marina three times over. He knew the boat had pulled in here. He'd seen it disappearing around the buoys marking the harbor and the marina. He'd practically burned up the motor of the speedboat to get here and see it, but he knew they'd brought the boat here. Only now the boat was gone, the rain had stopped and the curtain of night was suffocating him.

And they'd taken Gena and Scotty.

He could waste time searching the docks or he could ask questions, hoping someone had seen something.

Pulling up to the public dock, he decided he'd crack a few heads and get some answers. It was the only way. No one else was here to help him. Brice was back at his home in Atlanta and Devon was waiting to hear word back in Dixon. Kissie would do whatever she could, but she couldn't get here in time without endangering Scotty and Gena.

He was all alone. Lifting his head to the heavens, he stood as rain washed over him. "I need You, Lord. I need You. For Scotty's sake, not for mine." He stood, holding out his hands, palms up, praying to the God he'd turned away from so long ago. Praying for one last shred of salvation.

Then he headed up the boat ramp and stomped across the parking lot. There was a hotel right on the marina, mostly there for fishermen. He might be able to find out some information in the restaurant.

Soaking wet, he headed for the warmth of the building, asking questions here and there, describing the boat he'd seen, describing Gena and Scotty and the two men with them.

But no one inside had noticed anything out of the ordinary. No one had seen the four. And some of the fishermen started asking questions back, too many questions to suit Eli. He was making a scene and that wouldn't help Gena and Scotty.

He left, his skin crawling with dread, his mind overcome with a nasty feeling of déjà-vu, memories of another time when he'd been searching for his wife coming back to torment him. The only thing left to do was to scour the entire island for any sign of them. Unless they'd already taken them off the island. He'd search Barataria Pass and Caminada Bay if he had to, even the small island of Grand Terre across the sound. He'd search the entire ocean.

He'd find them. This time, he'd find his family.

When he saw an old pickup truck with kayaks loaded on steel racks on its bed, Eli flagged down the driver, trying to steady his breathing. "Hey. I could use a ride to the other side of the island. My boat's broke down and I have to get my truck."

The gray-haired man gave him the once over, then said, "Get in. You look liked a drowned rat."

"I feel that way," Eli said, shutting the door with a bang, searching for any conversation. "I was supposed to meet some friends, but I guess the storm scared them off."

"Yeah, well, did the same with my kayakers this afternoon, too."

Eli picked up on that. "Were you out just before the storm?"

"Nope. Had a scheduled outing, but it got too choppy. I had to send my takers home. We'll try again tomorrow. I sat here through the worst of the storm and now I want to get home and make a strong pot of coffee."

"Did you happen to see a small motorboat coming in? Black with gold stripes on each side. Two men and a woman and a little boy. They're my friends and I'm worried about them."

The man thought hard for a few seconds. "You know, come to think of it, I did see a group like that. The men had on wind pants and caps, but the kid was just about freezing—soaking wet even though he had on a light red jacket."

Eli had to turn and stare out the window to keep his cool. Scotty had a red jacket. "Dark haired kid about six or so?"

"Yep. And the woman had dark hair, too. She had on a long, brown jacket. She kinda nodded at me in passing."

"That had to be them," Eli replied, forcing a smile while his insides went icy and brittle. "At least I know they made it in safely."

"I wouldn't worry about 'em," the man said. "Don't know about the boat, but they got into a nice sleek black sedan. Must be with one of those big shots that rent out camp houses down here."

"*Oui,* that's it. I have to catch up with them."

"What's the name? I might know of 'em."

Eli grunted, shifted in his seat. "Can I be honest?"

The man centered him with a deadpan look. "I was waiting for that, yeah."

"The woman…she's my girlfriend. She left the house with my son and two men. I don't know their names. But her name is Gena."

The man gave him a doubtful look. "Look, mister, I don't want any trouble. All I know is they got in that big car. And they're probably long gone by now." He stopped the truck near a white church. "I live here by the church. This is as far as I go."

Eli nodded but pushed on. "I love this woman. And she has my son."

"You ain't one of them mean men who punch women, are you?"

Eli let out a breath, going on faith alone. "*Non,* they're in trouble. I need help, *mon ami.* I grew up on this island and brought them here to protect them, but they're in trouble. Real trouble."

The man's whole attitude changed then. "Well, why didn't you say so in the first place?"

Eli closed his eyes, precious seconds ticking by. "I have a hard time trusting people."

The man looked him over, then pointed to the church. "Go sit in there and get your thoughts together."

Eli grabbed him by his T-shirt. "I don't want the cops involved."

"No cops," the man replied. "We won't need them. All we need is the island grapevine. We'll find that car. But not if you don't let me go, right now."

Eli looked down at his fists clenched on the man's shirt. "Okay, but…I can't just sit here—"

"Yes, you can." The man pointed to the church again. "Go. Let me take things from here."

Eli nodded. "Hey, what's your name?"

"You first."

"Eli Trudeau."

"I'm Sandy. Sandy Kincaid. Nice to meet you."

"Same here."

"Now go on inside and get you a cup of coffee. I'll be back in a few minutes to let you know what I've found out."

Eli's first instinct was to push the man out of the way and take the truck. But something held him back. He had to think; he had to form a plan. So he turned and headed up the long church ramp to the open doors of the sanctuary.

A single light burned near the altar of the small, tidy room. That light looked like a beacon to Eli. He sank down on one of the oak pews and, closing his eyes, he began to pray.

EIGHTEEN

"Mommy, we're on a smelly boat."

Gena held Scotty close, the faint stench of stale seafood overwhelming her with each breath. "I know, honey. It's a shrimp boat." They were on a small bunk right across from the tiny galley just beyond the wheelhouse. Gena had already scoped the cabin for weapons and so far, she'd found spatulas, a few pots and pans and a stained coffeepot full of the syrupy dark brew. And some sort of Cajun spice mix that could possibly cause temporary blindness if she tossed it in someone's eyes.

"Mr. Eli said he used to work on shrimp boats. Think he'll find us here?"

"I hope so," she replied. And prayed so. "I'm sure he's trying right now." Gena kissed Scotty's dark curls and closed her eyes, her prayers centered on God's grace and reassurance. *I can take anything, Lord. Just protect my son.* Scotty didn't deserve this; he was innocent. So very innocent.

"How are you?"

Gena opened her eyes to find a man standing above them in the shadows. The night was moonless because of the cloud cover. But she knew who this man was. "Mr. Crane, let us go."

"Hello, Gena. I trust you're okay down here."

Gena swallowed the words that came to mind. "We're not okay. We need to go home."

"I can't allow that. I have to wait this out until Eli comes for you."

"How can he come when he doesn't know where we are?"

"He will soon enough, I'm sure."

Gena gasped as realization hit her with gale force. "You want him here."

"Of course, I do. Where would be the justice without his being here to beg for the boy's life? He's a smart man. He'll find you."

Gena held Scotty pinned against her. "Please…for my son's sake, think about what you're doing. Consider your words."

The man motioned to someone up on deck. "You're right, of course. Little ears and all of that." When the other man appeared, he said, "Take the boy."

"No!" Gena held Scotty to her. "Don't do this, please. This is not Eli's fault."

She was met with silence for a minute then, "But someone has to pay for what happened to my family and my business."

Another man came down the steps and Gena went into fight mode. Pushing up off the bunk, she grabbed for the pot full of steaming coffee and threw it into the man's startled face. He screamed and fell over on the floor.

Gena grabbed Scotty, trying to calm his sobs. "I won't let you take him."

"You'll regret that." Crane stomped down the stairs and yanked Gena so hard her head hit against the steel railing of the top bunk. "My daughter didn't have anyone to protect her. She was taken against her will and she died because of CHAIM. This upright organization that's supposed to do good work and help people killed *my* only child."

"So you're going to do the same here?" Gena looked from the black ring with the flashing yellow diamonds on his finger to the man's cold, blue eyes and saw a vast emptiness. He looked gaunt with grief, his eyes sunk back in his head as if already his flesh was falling away. "You can't punish an innocent child for something that happened long ago. It's not right."

"It's the only right I know," Crane said. "My wife left me and I've lost most of my fortune. It's the only right I know now." He motioned to the groaning man. "Take her to the shed."

Gena shrank back, but the man's anger made him snap her up with a death grip. "My pleasure, Mr. Crane."

"Don't do this," she pleaded. "Don't hurt him."

Scotty's sniffles sounded in the rocking boat. "Mommy!"

Gena's fear for her son radiated with a burning heat inside her body. Numb with nausea, she said, "It's okay, honey. This will be over soon, I promise."

"Yes, one way or another," Crane said. "You have a reprieve for now, but if you try any more tricks, things will only get worse. If you don't do exactly as I say, you will regret it." He walked over to Scotty. "Think about what that means."

Gena could think of nothing else as she watched Kenneth Crane holding her sobbing son.

He couldn't think past finding his son and Gena.

Eli faced the oak altar where a pedestal cross carved out of cypress stood behind an open Bible.

He tried to speak, tried to form the words, but his tears

were too close. Finally, he let out a shuddering sigh. "I need You, Lord. I need You here with me. I'm so weary, so tired. I turned away once, but I'm turning *to* You tonight. Don't make my family lost to me. Help me find my son and give him the kind of life I always wanted." He rubbed at his eyes, held his hands templed together as he bowed his head. "I love her, Lord. I love her and I want her to be with me always. Scotty needs his mother and his father." Eli looked up at the lamp burning so brightly in the dark chapel. "I need You in my life, Lord."

He sat silent for a few minutes, his mind whirling with longing as he thought about the grandfather who'd hated him enough to destroy him, of the father who'd never had the chance to love him, of his mother who'd suffered and died of a broken heart. And of his son, so special, so young and free and trusting.

And he thought of Gena. He knew she'd fight until death to save Scotty. What if he never saw her again? What if he had to accept that she was dead?

"I can't do that!" He got up to pace around the tiny sanctuary, his heart splintering with each agonized breath. "I can't allow that, Lord. I pray You won't allow that. No matter *my* sins, don't make them pay. Don't make them suffer."

He stumbled to a bench and went silent, spent and drained, waiting for the peace that only God could grant. And somehow, just like the storm outside, Eli calmed and stilled, praying that this time God would favor him with a new hope. He waited, his thoughts centered on his family. His new family.

In a few minutes, Sandy bounded through the door. "I think I found out where they took 'em, Eli."

Eli looked up at the altar. Then he rushed out the door with Sandy, determined to find Gena and Scotty.

"You're sure?"

"As sure as the sun's gonna come up tomorrow."

They stood just a few blocks down past the church, near a deserted shrimp shed located on an old bayside loading dock. A shrimp boat was floating in the water near the shed. Sandy assured him he had witnesses who'd seen the big sedan pull right up to that boat. Eli studied the quiet, abandoned dock. *"Merci, mon ami."*

Sandy grinned. "Go get 'em while I round up some muscle."

Eli nodded, then took off on foot toward the shrimp shed. The trawler was about forty-feet long with netting booms draped against the riggings like bat wings. Skirting around the dark shed, Eli listened for any noise. Two men appeared on the boat's deck. He'd check the shed first, then figure out how to get onto the boat.

He couldn't let that boat go out into deep waters.

Not without him on it.

It was too quiet.

Gena closed her eyes, centering her prayers on survival, her hope that Eli would find Scotty.

In the muted darkness of the shrimp shed, she tried to work at the ropes holding her hands behind her back. Gritting her teeth against the scream held underneath the tape they'd put across her mouth, she centered her mind on her son, her heart breaking with the image of him sobbing and calling her.

Then she heard a grunt and some scuffling noises near

the door. After a couple of minutes the darkness became deadly silence and still again. She *felt* him nearby before she actually saw him. Eli appeared above her, his silhouette rising up like a giant in the darkness.

"Chère?"

Gena dropped her head, a sob catching in her dry throat. Eli quickly worked the tape off her mouth. "They have Scotty on the boat," she said, tears running down her face.

He let out a sharp breath, then gathered her against his chest. "Are you all right?"

Gena nodded, the lump in her throat too great to speak above a whisper. "We have to get out of here and get Scotty. They were waiting for you."

"Oui, of that I have no doubt. Well, I'm here now. And we have one less guard to worry about."

Then they heard footsteps, slow and sure, hitting on the cracked concrete. "Eli Trudeau, as I live and breathe."

Eli started to turn.

"Don't do anything foolish. We have your son out on the boat. Mighty deep water out past the wake. Hope he's a good swimmer."

Eli hissed a breath, but he didn't move. "Let the boy go, Crane. You have me now."

"Can't oblige. I need Mrs. Thornton to help me locate some files. And I need the boy as collateral to assure she'll cooperate. She's going to find what I'm looking for and make it go away, or your son will go away."

Eli glanced past Crane, sure he had more guards. Then he moved toward Gena, hoping to free her somehow, his mind working on saving his son.

"Let's get started," Crane said. He opened his cell phone and hit numbers. "Take the boat out toward the dropoff."

Eli's heart hammered at the sound of the engine revving. "Don't do this, Crane. We can end this now without hurting Gena or the boy."

Crane ignored him. He looked at Gena. "I have a computer over there by the counting board. And I have the equipment to make it run. It's up to you to break down the codes and find the files Savoy hid from me—files that could ruin me for good. If you don't find them in the hard drive by midnight, you won't see your son again."

Gena gulped in a breath. "I don't have that kind of knowledge. I can't—"

"You can and you will. I've kept tabs on you all these years. You'll figure it out."

Eli stepped forward, but two heavily armed men met him. "Let me go to my son," he said.

"You're willing to leave her here?"

Gena glared up at him. "Yes, he is. I'll do as you ask, but you have to promise me you won't hurt Scotty."

Eli added to that. "Let me go stay with Scotty. He's scared. He's just a little boy." He gave Gena an apologetic look.

"Don't worry about me," she said, her meaning clear. She wanted him to find Scotty.

Crane motioned to the men. "Sorry, Trudeau, I can't do that. I'm sick and tired of Pierre Savoy and all his manipulations. The man ruined me and now you have to suffer the consequences. Once we're done here, you'll finally vanish off the face of the earth and I'll be able to find some peace."

The men untied Gena and took her over to the table near the board where shrimp were weighed and counted. "Get started."

Crane motioned to Eli. "I think we'd better tie him up good and tight. He's as slippery as an eel."

They took him near the ramp that ran on a conveyor belt, pushing him into a chair so that they could restrain him. And for the first time that night, Eli breathed a sigh of relief, because he knew a thing or two about shrimp sheds and conveyor belts.

An hour later, Gena dropped her head against her hands. "I can't find anything. You should understand that. This is your system."

Crane huffed a breath. "An hour until midnight. You'd better try again."

Eli had been struggling at the ropes around his wrists. If he could break free and hit the conveyor belt at least it would give him time to take one of the men. And his mind had been at work, too. And like a flash of lightning everything became crystal clear. He had the code Crane was looking for—his grandfather had purposely left it. While he undid the ropes, he came up with a plan.

"Hey, Crane, I found a picture of you and my grandfather. It had some funny numbers on the back."

Crane came toward Eli, his hand outstretched. "Give it to me!"

Eli shot Gena a look, smiled, and said "I'd like nothing better, but I'm a bit tied up at the moment." With a long sigh, he told Crane where the picture was.

If he was wrong, well, this would at least be a distraction. "Try these numbers and letters, Gena."

Crane stared at the picture, then shoved it at Gena. "Get on with it."

Gena's gaze slammed into Eli's, her expression bordering on disbelief. "Go ahead, *chère*. Make it *vanish*. Send it away. You know, like when we were at the safe house. It's just a system."

Gena's expression changed and she nodded. "I think I know how to do that."

Eli waited while she keyed in the numbers and letters. Crane watched over her shoulder, his expression a mixture of fascination and disgust as she hit buttons and deleted documents. "Now that wasn't so hard, was it? And twenty minutes to spare."

Gena shook her head. "No." Then she turned to stare up at him. "Now bring me back my child."

Eli grunted. "We did what you asked. And now we're done playing games." Then he threw off the ropes and hit the conveyor belt switch. The grinding noise caused the two guards to come running as Crane stepped back in surprise.

Eli didn't waste time. He lifted his lower body and kicked Crane square in the stomach, causing the man to fall to the floor. Then Eli rammed right into one of the guards, knocking down the man and his gun. Eli kicked the gun into the dark. As the guard who'd been standing over Gena reached to grab her, she lifted the laptop and with a mighty whack, hit him up beside the head. He went down with a grunt.

Eli grabbed a crab trap off the wall and hauled it up toward the guard on the floor, jabbing the man with the wire mesh. After finding both guns, he put one at his waist and came back to where Crane lay writhing on the floor then reached inside Crane's windbreaker for his cell phone. "I have two guns, and one's centered on you. Call the boat and tell them to *bring my son*."

Crane managed a chuckle. "Go ahead and kill me. Then you'll never see your son again."

Eli pressed the gun to his chest. "I won't kill you, Crane. But I will tell you this—Gena deleted your files, but if I know her, she saved a copy of everything and routed it right into CHAIM's hands. I'll make sure the authorities get that information. You won't die, but you'll sure wish you did. Give me my son and I'll make it all go away again."

Crane looked ill, but he barked out a number. When Eli had a response he put the phone to Crane's ear, then whispered, "Tell them to bring him back."

Crane mumbled into the phone, then dropped his head back to the floor. Eli handed Gena the other gun. "Watch him."

Gena's hand was steady on the weapon as she stood over Crane. Eli went to work on the two guards, then turned back toward Crane and watched as the man lifted off the floor and rushed Gena, struggling to take the gun.

She screamed and went down underneath him. Eli ran toward them as a gun shot rang out. Crane rolled and brought Gena up with him. When she slumped against him, Eli rushed forward and saw blood spilling out over her sweater.

"She's hurt!" Eli said, lurching forward toward Gena.

Crane put the gun close to her head. "But she's still alive. If you come any nearer, I'll finish it. Follow me out to the dock."

Crane pushed Gena up to the swirling water. She tried to keep from passing out, her hand going to her shoulder as blood seeped through her fingers.

"I'll make a deal with you, Trudeau. It's too late for me now because you sent that file to CHAIM, but not too late to make you pay for that trick. When the boat gets here, you can choose which one will live or die."

Gena shook her head, her whisper weak. "Eli..."

"I can't do that," Eli said, his eyes on Gena, willing her to hang on. "I can't make that choice. You see, I love both of them."

"Then I'll make it for you," Crane said. "You wanted to find the boy. I don't think you'll miss *her* too much."

Gena didn't have to see Eli's face to know the horror of what this man was asking. "Eli, help Scotty. Please, Eli."

Crane words grinded in her ear. "This is what happened to my little girl. I've been waiting a long time for justice."

Eli stepped closer. "My grandfather did you wrong, but—"

Crane shoved Gena toward the water. "You can't save her."

Gena looked at Eli. "Remember you promised me—you said you'd always take care of Scotty. Do that. For me." She gulped back a sob, her gaze centered on him. "If you love me, Eli, you will do this for me."

Eli's heart was breaking. He couldn't let this madman kill Gena. "Crane, please," he said, hoping the man would find compassion somewhere in his twisted heart. "Kill me and get it over with, but let her go."

"I don't want *you*," Crane replied. "I'm going to take someone *you* love. You and your grandfather killed my daughter. Now it's payback time."

Eli sucked in a breath, closing his eyes to the grief shattering his last hold on reality. He felt as if the whole world had turned dark, as if he was facing this evil alone in a great wilderness.

He looked at Gena, saw the plea there in her eyes. *"Vous êtes mon coeur."*

Gena's tears fell freely, wetting Crane's hand near her cheek. "No, Eli, *he* is your heart. He's always been your heart." She swallowed. "I'll be okay."

Eli clenched his teeth. "No."

Crane's chuckle clinked like glass. "The lady has spoken. She's ready to make a sacrifice."

Off in the distance, Eli heard a boat's purring motor. "Crane, wait."

But Crane was beyond pleas. He turned Gena toward the dark water and with a grunt, pushed her into the bay.

Eli ran toward the water, screaming her name. "Gena!"

Crane pushed him, the gun in his face. "You get to keep *your* child, Trudeau. And you can explain to him how you watched his mother die. Twice. And I can die laughing at you, because I killed both of the boy's mothers. You see, that information is what I was trying to destroy."

Eli went sick inside. Crane had been the one to go after Leah—on his grandfather's orders. He looked down the barrel pointed at his forehead and welcomed the cold steel, welcomed a quick death, a release. But the thought of leaving Scotty all alone shattered the darkness swirling around him. "You have made a grave mistake."

"I don't think so," Crane said. "I'm the one holding the gun."

Eli grunted, all of the rage he'd felt for so many years merging into a storm of overwhelming, consuming anger. "I will not lose her and I will not lose my son."

With that, he pushed toward the gun, using all of his strength to force Crane's arm up into the air. Because the other man was already winded and not nearly as strong, Eli took advantage and managed to subdue him. Then he lifted the gun out of Crane's craggy fingers, ready to kill the man on the spot.

But the boat was coming toward the shore. And his son was on it. And Gena hadn't come up out of the water yet.

He pushed past the burning haze of pain and grief, sending a silent plea to God to show him the way.

And then lights suddenly flared all over the deserted parking lot. Eli held Crane, then looked around to find Sandy Kincaid and a passel of islanders walking toward him.

"We came to stop this tempest," one of the men said. "We don't like outsiders causing trouble on our island."

Eli wanted to weep with relief, but instead, he went into action. "Gena's been shot and she's in the water."

Sandy bobbed his head. "We'll take care of him. Go! Go!"

"My son's on that boat," Eli called. "I have to find him." Then he jumped into the water. The cold depth hit him, taking him down into a blackness that gave no quarter. With a sheer force of will, he managed to surface a few feet from where Gena had gone in. "Gena? Gena?"

The boat was easing up to the dock now. Eli swam around it to the landing past the seawall. "Gena?"

Hitting the water with his hands, he thought about how much he loved her. "I don't think I can bear this," he whispered. Then he heard a splashing sound near the back of the big trawler. And saw a flash of long, dark hair.

"Gena?"

"Eli," she called, weak but alive. "I'm going on that boat to get my son. Are you coming?"

About twenty minutes later, they had Scotty and they were back on the dock, Eli carrying Gena in his arms while Scotty held on to Eli's pants, hurrying to keep up with him. "It's okay, son. We have to get your *maman* to a doctor."

Five big, burly men and one skinny white-haired one surrounded Kenneth Crane with shotguns. "It's over for you now, mister," one of the men said, grinning.

How Sandy managed to round them all up at this hour was beyond Eli. But then, this island had its own kind of law and its own code of decency.

One of the men, a giant with hands the size of sea turtles, stepped up to Eli. "You want us to finish this for you, *frère?*" He pounded one of his meaty fists into his other palm. "Where you want us to dump him? The bay or the sea, or maybe in some alligator-infested marsh?"

Eli shook his head, his eyes on Gena as he kept walking. "Call 911. She's been shot. Then call the police and let them handle the rest. I'll be waiting at the church for the ambulance."

Sandy pulled out his cell phone. "She gonna make it?"

"She is."

Eli kissed her, brushing at her hair. "It's over."

"Scotty," she said through chattering teeth.

"We have him, love. You have your son."

"And so do you," she whispered. Then she passed out.

Days later, Eli sat with Scotty near Gena's bed. Sandy had offered them his house to use while Gena recuperated and while Eli gave his statement to the authorities and made sure Kenneth Crane was locked up for good.

"Look," he said to Scotty. "The sunset is coming."

Scotty stretched, his eyes wide with curiosity. "Can we stay here awhile—on the island? I like it here."

Gena, her wound clean and bandaged, sent Eli a worried

look. "But a lot happened here, Scotty. And we have to get ready for Devon and Lydia's wedding."

Scotty shifted on the settee next to Eli, his tiny hand touching Eli's. "Are you coming to the wedding?"

Eli ruffled his hair. "For sure."

Scotty grinned, then lowered his head. "You called me son, remember? When we had to get Mom to the hospital?"

Eli cast out a worried frown. "I think I do remember." He looked at Gena for guidance. She nodded, her eyes misty. "Is that okay, that I called you that?"

Scotty looked up at him, his dark eyes mirroring those of his father. "Does that mean you're my dad?"

Gena reached out a hand. "Would you like that?"

Scotty bobbed his head. "I was kind of hoping…"

Eli gave his son a level gaze. "We'll figure all of that out, all in good time. With some church counselors helping us along the way. We have a lot to work through." Then he took Scotty onto his lap. "But I can tell you this—I would love to be your dad."

That seemed to satisfy Scotty. He got up to go out onto the little porch so he could watch the waves crashing on the other side of the dunes.

Eli turned to Gena. "And how do you feel about that, *catin?*"

Gena's gaze held his, then she reached up to touch his face. "First, how do you feel? I mean, now that we know the truth?"

Eli thought about Leah, about how his grandfather had used Crane to get even with him. He loved her still and he mourned her still. But Gena and Scotty needed him now. And he needed them. "I'm gonna make it, *chère*. I'm gonna make it."

"Can you live with the truth now?"

He saw the worry darkening her eyes. "Yes. I have to live with a lot, but I also have a lot to live for."

Her smile trembled. "We'll get you through it, Eli, because I know I *can't* live without you. I love you."

Eli pulled her into his arms. "I love you, too." He held back, looking at her. "I never thought I'd say that again to a woman, but…I love you and I love our son. And I'll take care of you both, always."

Gena's eyes sparkled. "We're going to be a family."

"*Oui,* at long last." He took her hands in his. "And you know where I want to go on our honeymoon?"

"We're getting married?"

"*Oui,* that makes a family, right?"

She nodded, her smile captivating. "Yes. So…where do you want to go on our honeymoon?"

"Maine."

She burst out laughing. "But you hate the cold."

He kissed her, then stayed close. Touching his heart, he said, "I'm not so cold anymore."

Gena returned his kiss. "Are you sure you want to go back to Maine?"

He let her long hair trail through his fingers. "*Oui,* but maybe in the spring."

* * * * *

Dear Reader,

This book was both a joy and a torment to write. I fell in love with Eli Trudeau the minute he popped into my head, but I knew his story would be hard to write. The whole idea of writing stories about Christians who are also part of an elite secret society that tries to take care of fellow Christians all over the world was a big challenge and Eli's story was definitely part of that challenge. Eli suffered so much growing up without a father and then finding a grandfather who hated him and used him in such an evil way. But the good news, of course, is that Eli turned to God to help him make his life different.

When Eli meets Gena and finally comes face-to-face with the son he never knew, his hard heart softens bit by bit and he realizes that when he thought he was in that desolate place, all alone and grieving, God was right there with him, helping him to become a better man. He is put to the test when he has to save his son and the woman who has been raising him. But Gena's love and loyalty wins Eli's heart. For once, someone believes in Eli and that gives him the courage to finally give his heart to God and to the woman he loves.

I hope you enjoyed this story and I hope you'll look for the next installment of my CHAIM series—*Code of Honor*, due out later this year. While we might not have secret agents watching out for us when we're in trouble, we do have God's love and abiding grace. I hope you reach out for that love and grace in your own life so you can come out of your desolate place.

Visit me at www.lenoraworth.com. I love hearing from readers.

Until next time…

May the angels watch over you. Always.

Lenora Worth

QUESTIONS FOR DISCUSSION

1. Why was it so important for Eli to find Scotty? Do you believe he made the right choice?

2. Why was Gena so afraid of what Eli might do? How did she learn to trust him?

3. Do you believe Gena's faith helped her to cope with the possibility of losing Scotty? Did it help her to soften toward Eli?

4. What was the turning point for Eli? Why did he decide not to take Scotty away from Gena?

5. Have you known people who've searched for lost relatives, only to be disappointed or disillusioned? How can God's love help in that situation?

6. Why did Eli think Scotty was in danger? Have you ever felt as if something bad was going to happen but you weren't sure what?

7. Why do you think Devon (Gena's brother) turned Scotty over to her? Do you think she was the best choice to raise Scotty?

8. Do you believe sometimes we have to make a sacrifice in order to protect those we love? Has this happened in your life?

9. Do you think it's right to seek retribution for a past mistake? Why did Eli believe this was going to happen with him?

10. Did Eli do the right thing, taking Scotty and Gena on the run? What else could he have done?

11. Why was Eli's grandfather so against Eli? Have you known people who can't get past their prejudice to open their hearts to love? How can God help in this situation?

12. Why did Eli go back to Grand Isle? Have you ever had to go back to a place that holds both good and bad memories for you?

13. Gena fought for Scotty with a mother's love. Why is that so important? How does that parallel with God's love for us?

14. What choice did Eli have to make in the end in order to save Scotty? Do you think he made the right choice?

15. Eli turned to God in the tiny chapel because he was back in that desolate place. How did that decision help him? Have you turned to God in times of despair?

Love Inspired
HISTORICAL

*Powerful, engaging stories of romance, adventure
and faith set in the past—when things were simpler
and faith played a major role in everyday lives.*

Turn the page for a sneak preview of
THE MAVERICK PREACHER
by
Victoria Bylin

*Love Inspired Historical—love and faith
throughout the ages*

Mr. Blue looked into her eyes with silent understanding and she wondered if he, too, had a struggled with God's ways. The slash of his brow looked tight with worry, and his whiskers were too stubbly to be permanent. Adie thought about his shaving tools and wondered when he'd used them last. Her new boarder would clean up well on the outside, but his heart remained a mystery. She needed to keep it that way. The less she knew about him, the better.

"Good night," she said. "Bessie will check you in the morning."

"Before you go, I've been wondering…"

"About what?"

"The baby… Who's the mother?"

Adie raised her chin. "I am."

Earlier he'd called her "Miss Clarke" and she hadn't corrected him. The flash in his eyes told her that he'd assumed she'd given birth out of wedlock. Adie resented being judged, but she counted it as the price of protecting Stephen. If Mr. Blue chose to condemn her, so be it. She'd done nothing for which to be ashamed. With their gazes locked, she waiting for the criticism that didn't come.

Instead he laced his fingers on top of the Bible. "Children are a gift, all of them."

"I think so, too."

He lightened his tone. "A boy or a girl?"

"A boy."

The man smiled. "He sure can cry. How old is he?"

Adie didn't like the questions at all, but she took pride in her son. "He's three months old." She didn't mention that he'd been born six weeks early. "I hope the crying doesn't disturb you."

"I don't care if it does."

He sounded defiant. She didn't understand. "Most men would be annoyed."

"The crying's better than silence…. I know."

Adie didn't want to care about this man, but her heart fluttered against her ribs. What did Joshua Blue know of babies and silence? Had he lost a wife? A child of his own? She wanted to express sympathy but couldn't. If she pried into his life, he'd pry into hers. He'd ask questions and she'd have to hide the truth. *Stephen was born too soon and his mother died. He barely survived. I welcome his cries, every one of them. They mean he's alive.*

With a lump in her throat, she turned to leave. "Good night, Mr. Blue."

"Good night."

A thought struck her and she turned back to his room. "I suppose I should call you Reverend."

He grimaced. "I'd prefer Josh."

* * * * *

*Don't miss this deeply moving Love Inspired Historical
story about a man of God who's lost his way
and the woman who helps him rediscover his faith—
and his heart.*
THE MAVERICK PREACHER
by Victoria Bylin
available February 2009.

And also look for
THE MARSHAL TAKES A BRIDE
by Renee Ryan,
*in which a lawman meets his match in a feisty
schoolteacher with marriage on her mind.*

REQUEST YOUR FREE BOOKS!

2 FREE RIVETING INSPIRATIONAL NOVELS
PLUS 2 FREE MYSTERY GIFTS

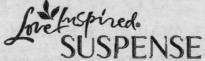

YES! Please send me 2 FREE Love Inspired® Suspense novels and my 2 FREE mystery gifts (gifts are worth about $10). After receiving them, if I don't wish to receive any more books, I can return the shipping statement marked "cancel". If I don't cancel, I will receive 4 brand-new novels every month and be billed just $4.24 per book in the U.S. or $4.74 per book in Canada, plus 25¢ shipping and handling per book and applicable taxes, if any*. That's a savings of over 20% off the cover price! I understand that accepting the 2 free books and gifts places me under no obligation to buy anything. I can always return a shipment and cancel at any time. Even if I never buy another book, the two free books and gifts are mine to keep forever.

123 IDN ERXX   323 IDN ERXM

Name	(PLEASE PRINT)	
Address		Apt. #
City	State/Prov.	Zip/Postal Code

Signature (if under 18, a parent or guardian must sign)

Order online at www.LoveInspiredSuspense.com
Or mail to Steeple Hill Reader Service:

IN U.S.A.: P.O. Box 1867, Buffalo, NY 14240-1867
IN CANADA: P.O. Box 609, Fort Erie, Ontario L2A 5X3

Not valid to current subscribers of Love Inspired Suspense books.

Want to try two free books from another series?
Call 1-800-873-8635 or visit www.morefreebooks.com

* Terms and prices subject to change without notice. N.Y. residents add applicable sales tax. Canadian residents will be charged applicable provincial taxes and GST. Offer not valid in Quebec. This offer is limited to one order per household. All orders subject to approval. Credit or debit balances in a customer's account(s) may be offset by any other outstanding balance owed by or to the customer. Please allow 4 to 6 weeks for delivery. Offer available while quantities last.

Your Privacy: Steeple Hill Books is committed to protecting your privacy. Our Privacy Policy is available online at www.SteepleHill.com or upon request from the Reader Service. From time to time we make our lists of customers available to reputable third parties who may have a product or service of interest to you. If you would prefer we not share your name and address, please check here. ☐

LISUS08R

Love Inspired®
SUSPENSE

TITLES AVAILABLE NEXT MONTH

Don't miss these four stories on sale February 10, 2009

ON A KILLER'S TRAIL by Susan Page Davis
When a sweet, elderly lady is found dead on Christmas Day, rookie reporter Kate Richards jumps on the story. Detective Neil Alexander can't figure out the murderer's motive, but he _does_ know that Kate needs watching. They're on a killer's trail. And who knows what they'll find....

FRAMED! by Robin Caroll
Without a Trace
The prime suspect in her brother's murder: Max Pershing, the man Ava Renault has always secretly loved. To help Max, she'll have to overcome their feuding families and expose the truth.

EVIDENCE OF MURDER by Jill Elizabeth Nelson
The photographs Samantha Reid uncovers in her new store could be deadly. They present new insight into a cold case _someone_ wants to keep closed. And when Samantha is pushed into the spotlight, Ryan Davidson—sole survivor of the slain family—must intervene to keep her safe.

DEADLY REUNION by Florence Case
Her sister's engaged to a murderer. Police officer Angie Delitano is convinced of it. Then Angie uncovers startling new evidence, forcing her to turn to Boone, the handsome, hardened lawyer she once loved. Now she has to learn to trust him again—with the case and with her heart.

LISCNMBPA0109